THE CANADIAN FALL

By Mitchell Lanigan

Dear Reader,

Some stories unfold gently. This is not one of them.

The Canadian Fall is a novel about power, choices, and the quiet manipulations that shape our lives when we aren't looking. It's about marriage — not the kind that sparkles under the spotlight, but the kind that suffocates behind closed doors. It's also about love — the kind that twists, corrodes, and leaves you wondering if you ever really had it.

Ann McFadden was never meant to be the perfect wife. Yet, somewhere between the promises and the silences, she became one. She let go of her career, choices, and voice until a single moment shattered the illusion. When a woman falls to her death, reality starts unraveling, forcing Ann to ask the one question she has spent years avoiding: What role has she played in her own undoing?

At the heart of this novel is a mystery — not just who killed who, but who holds the power in our relationships and what happens when the balance shifts. Every character is hiding something. Every conversation is laced with meaning. And when the truth finally emerges, it may not be the truth you expected. Or the whole truth at all.

Are you ready for the fall?

PROLOGUE

Early December mornings in Toronto are the worst—an unwelcoming limbo between autumn and winter, where the air is thick with damp cold, clinging to the skin like an unshaken sense of dread. The sky, an oppressive shade of dark gray, looms over the city, pregnant with the promise of snow that stubbornly refuses to fall before Christmas. Wind tumbles off the lake, curling through the streets, seeping into collars and cuffs, turning breaths into fleeting ghosts. It's a morning meant for staying in, for lingering under warm covers, for waiting out the season's indecision.

But the city never waits.
Rush hour creeps forward, sluggish but relentless. Headlights blur through the mist. Car horns sputter half-hearted protests. Somewhere, a siren wails, distant, disinterested. The streets pulse with movement, a slow, synchronized march of commuters clutching their Tim Hortons cups like lifelines, the steam rising in desperate wisps.

At a busy intersection, a small crowd clusters at the curb, waiting for the light to change. Their faces are drawn, indifferent, minds already trapped inside spreadsheets and inboxes. The towering glass monolith of the office building ahead looms over them, swallowing the weak morning light, its steel edges slicing into the sky. A place of deals and deadlines, of long hours under fluorescent buzz.

The light turns green.
The crowd moves forward, a current of wool coats and briefcases, heads bowed against the wind. No one looks up. No one ever looks up.
Then, a sound—deep, visceral, wrong. A sickening crack of metal bending, glass exploding, air being forced violently aside. A human body, a blur in freefall, slams into the roof of a parked car with a force so final, so absolute, that for a moment, no one moves. The impact is deafening, sending out a ripple of silence before the world remembers how to react.

A woman screams. Someone stumbles backward, hand over mouth. A man drops his coffee, brown liquid splattering onto frozen pavement. Others shrink away, instinctively shielding themselves from a horror they've already witnessed. The car's roof caves inward, crumpled like an empty can, shattered glass glittering over the wreckage.

The body, a woman, lies sprawled across the ruins of metal and glass, limbs twisted unnaturally, hair fanned out like ink spilled across a canvas. There is no movement. No sound.

She is impossibly still.

For a moment, there is nothing but stunned, breathless shock. Then, as if waking from a collective trance, hands fumble for phones, voices rise in frantic murmurs.

"Oh my God."
"Did she, did she fall?"
"Jesus Christ."
"Someone call 911!"

A siren wails closer, sharp and immediate, slicing through the chaos. Two police cruisers skid to a stop, doors flying open, uniforms spilling onto the street. Officers push forward, clearing bystanders, establishing control over the unraveling scene.

Another pair of officers corral the closest witnesses, ushering them into the lobby of the towering building, their expressions grim. These people saw it happen. They will be questioned.

They will be asked for details they wish they didn't have.

And the woman who fell from the sky stays behind. She is beyond saving.

Some people turn away, unable to stomach the sight. Others, transfixed, stare as if trying to make sense of the impossible. But one undeniable truth lingers in the freezing air, thick and suffocating. This December morning, so ordinary just hours ago, has been rewritten, warped into something dark, something irreversible. And high above the crowd, a window yawns open, the cold creeping in like an uninvited guest.

PART ONE: THE BLONDE

Chapter 1

"I fucking hate it," Ann muttered under her breath, pulling the door shut behind her with just enough force to make her point without actually slamming it. Spike tugged eagerly on his leash, blissfully oblivious to her simmering rage. What exactly she hated at that moment—her in-laws, the house, the entire neighborhood—was hard to pinpoint. Probably all of it. The suffocating combination.

Spike, on the other hand, was ecstatic. His tail wagged with the unbridled enthusiasm of a creature whose only expectation for the day was a cavalcade of glorious smells.

Ann used to love autumn. Crisp air, golden leaves, and the scent of woodsmoke curling through the streets. Now, the cold felt sharper, cutting through something fragile inside her. Maybe the season hadn't changed overnight. Maybe it had been shifting for years, and she just hadn't noticed. That was the thing about slow decay—you never saw it happening. Not until something snapped.

She walked faster, as if distance could loosen the invisible grip of the house behind her. She wouldn't call it home. It was a stage where she played the perfect wife under the watchful eyes of her in-laws—her mother-in-law's quiet disapproval, her father-in-law's heavy silence. Out here, she could breathe.

Spike bounded forward, nose to the ground, already lost in something profound—perhaps last night's gourmet leftovers tossed into a pristine compost bin. Ann smiled faintly. For the next hour and a half, this would be her time, too, the only part of the day that belonged solely to her. Spike had become her escape. Not that he knew it, of course.

Mark, Ann's husband, was a man obsessed with appearances. His entire world was built on a carefully crafted façade, polished to perfection, not for himself, but to dazzle anyone who happened to be watching. Success wasn't only something he relentlessly pursued. It was also something he flawlessly performed. Symbols meant everything to him.

Yes, those fucking symbols, Ann thought. The proper neighborhoods, the right friends, the right restaurants, the right jobs, the whole damn image of a perfect life. Two kids, a trophy wife, and now, a dog to complete the picture.

.

Oh yes, a dog, she almost murmured to herself. That was a big one for Mark. He spun it into some sentimental fantasy about family life, insisting a dog was essential, a hallmark of domestic bliss. Ann resisted with all her might, but in the end, he wore her down.

Her revenge was simple. And delicious.

When the time came to choose, she picked the ugliest dog she could find. Spike — wiry fur, uneven ears, a permanently disgruntled expression — was nothing like the glossy golden retriever Mark had envisioned. He'd been furious. That quiet, seething kind of furious that made it even better. But then something unexpected happened. The kids adored Spike. Within days, he was sleeping at the foot of their beds, proudly accompanying them on walks, greeting them with uncontainable joy every morning. He had cemented his place in the family, and even Ann couldn't help but grow fond of him. As for Mark, he tolerated Spike with the resigned air of a man who'd lost a battle he didn't know he was fighting.

"Battles, battles, battles," Ann whispered under her breath as she turned off the street onto the narrow nature trail that wound its way behind the neighborhood. Her life had become one long, silent battle. She never imagined marriage would feel like this—a war fought with no sound, no referee, and no visible wounds. She hadn't chosen Mark so much as she'd been chosen by him. It was her looks, of course. She wasn't classically beautiful—her features were too sharp for that—but she was unforgettable. Stunning in the way a lightning bolt slicing through the night is stunning. Tall, slim, effortlessly blonde, with a confidence she hadn't entirely earned but wore well enough. She was the trophy wife Mark always wanted, and he had closed the deal like the seasoned negotiator he was.

And what a deal it had been. The adoring fiancé, the extravagant wedding, the grand promises whispered into her ear when no one else was listening. Then, as if on cue, the curtain dropped. The applause faded. The show was over.
Now, it was just the routine—her in the house with the kids, his parents hovering like ghosts,

and Mark in Toronto, chasing lawyer glory and sketching new goals on an ever-distant horizon. For him, marriage was a box checked off his list. For Ann, it was a choice she never really made but couldn't seem to escape.

Eight years ago, her world had felt wide open. Nearly thirty, shifting jobs, leaving a corporate bank for a smaller, better-paying financial firm — a step up, though not a dream. Finance had never thrilled her, but her father once said, "People who work with other people's money are never poor." It stuck. She was good with numbers, so she followed the money, worked hard, moved up quickly, and earned enough to survive Toronto's daylight robbery of a rental market.

Then came Mark.

A lawyer, handling some dull case for the bank. She barely noticed him until the next day when a bouquet appeared on her desk with a note in crisp handwriting:

Lunch at Sassafraz. 12:30. See you there.

Bold. Unexpected. Exciting.
She went, of course. One lunch turned into two, then five, then weekend getaways and

extravagant gestures that made her feel like the center of his universe. Mark had relentless charm, and Ann let herself fall.

Then, after the honeymoon, everything stopped. No flowers. No surprise dinners. No thoughtful notes.

Mark, the man who had pursued her so persistently, had vanished, replaced by someone who saw her as an afterthought.

She rationalized it at first. Maybe stress. Maybe the weight of marriage settling in. She kept waiting for another surprise, another whispered promise. It never came.

***

Up ahead, Ann spotted him. The man with the dog. They crossed paths often, yet she had never spoken to him, never returned his polite nods. But today she couldn't ignore him. A few days ago, she had seen him differently.

Her in-laws had left early for Niagara, and the house had been unusually quiet. For once, she had lingered over breakfast, moving at her own pace, untethered from their scrutiny. Instead of their usual trail, she had taken Spike down to the lake. The sky had been sharp and blue, the water gleaming in the late-morning sun.

That's where she saw him.

He sat alone on a bench beneath an old oak tree, his dog curled at his feet. She wouldn't have thought much of it until she heard him speaking. Not in the usual, affectionate way people spoke to their pets. No teasing, no exaggerated baby talk. His voice was low, serious, almost... urgent. The words weren't in English. Some European language, smooth and melodic, yet weighed down by something unsaid. She hadn't understood a word. She hadn't needed to. There had been something in his tone, a quiet confession meant for no one but the dog.

She had lingered just long enough to feel intrusive, then kept walking. But the moment stayed, nagging at her. A private grief witnessed by accident.

And now, here he was again, heading toward her on the trail, his stride steady, his black lab trotting beside him. She even knew where he lived—just a few doors down, across from her in-laws' house. He had moved in three years ago, but she had carefully avoided neighbors. Now, though, she found herself looking. As he passed, he gave his usual polite nod, the faintest trace of a smile. But this time, she nodded back. Barely a movement, a flicker of acknowledgment. For the first time, she really saw his eyes. Deep brown.

Soft but heavy. Like a lake in late autumn — vast, still, carrying an ache beneath the surface. She paused, holding Spike back as he attempted to splash into a muddy puddle, her gaze following the man as he disappeared down the trail. Tall — definitely six feet. Slim, athletic. Tennis, maybe. Or Squash. Late forties, she guessed. He carried himself with the quiet confidence of someone who once had things figured out but had been dealt too many blows since. A strange feeling washed over her. An urge she couldn't explain. She wanted to call out, stop him, tell him she could listen if he needed someone. She could lend him her ear, maybe even open her soul if it helped. But then Spike yanked impatiently on the leash. She hissed at him for his unruly behavior, turning back toward the trail with a sharp tug, shaking off the fleeting impulse. She had her own problems, after all. Why on earth would she take on someone else's?

***

Ann dialed Jack, her younger brother, desperate for a distraction — from the man on the trail, from Mark, from everything. She needed a lifeline, a conversation, anything to switch gears. No luck. Jack's phone was off. Voicemail. She shoved her iPhone back into her pocket and turned her attention to Spike. A thought flashed—if Jack had answered, would she have admitted how she really felt? She let the question hang unanswered.

Focus on the walk. At least she could enjoy the fall. The leaves had just begun their slow transformation, painting the trees in amber, gold, and crimson, a final masterpiece before winter's long sleep. Ann let the beauty wash over her, steadying her restless mind. Right. She could at least enjoy the fall before returning to that haunted house. She had no way of knowing, at that moment, just how cruel the universe could be. Just how literal that word, fall, would become.

Her peace with nature was fleeting. The thoughts crept back in, weaving through her mind like unwelcome guests. Her focus drifted to the coming weekend—the dreaded wine-tasting trip to Niagara with Mark's colleagues and their wives. Trophies, too, of course. Ann hated these gatherings. She felt out of place, living a life that wasn't hers, trapped in conversations that meant nothing. The next milestone. The next pay raise. The next bonus. Endless chatter about court proceedings and ambitious goals spiraling higher and higher, as if chasing some unreachable summit. She didn't belong there. She never had.

***

The walk was over, and Ann was back at the front door. She guided Spike in, bending to wipe his paws— another unspoken rule of this house. She inspected them carefully, making sure they were clean enough to pass her mother-in-law's rigorous standards for her gleaming floors. As Ann crouched, towel in hand, Grace appeared in the kitchen doorway. A flicker of disapproval crossed her face. Her gaze darted to Spike's paws, then back to Ann. Satisfied, or maybe not, Grace disappeared without a word.

Bitch, Ann thought, but she kept her mouth shut. "What time are you picking up the kids?" Grace called from the kitchen, her voice sharp enough to carry upstairs.

"Same," Ann replied flatly, already halfway to the kids' room. She closed the door behind her, pretending to tidy up—straightening bedsheets and tossing toys into boxes. In reality, she scrolled through her phone, killing time before the school run.

Ann had left her career behind long ago. Mark and his parents had made it clear: Ann's job was unnecessary.

Unnecessary—that was their word for it. His parents had no interest in stepping in to help with the kids, but they strongly preferred Ann handle everything herself. His father had even offered to "throw in" extra cash to sweeten the deal as if she were some underpaid household employee. He, of course, kept himself locked in his study, glued to his enormous screen—tracking investments, checking market trends, and, occasionally, scrambling to close a Pornhub tab whenever footsteps approached.

When he wasn't watching stocks, he was watching something else. His other great preoccupation was his telescope. Aimed at the night sky—or, as Ann had noticed more than once, angled toward the neighbors' windows.

Twenty minutes before leaving for school pickup, Ann walked into the kitchen and put the kettle on. Grace was nearby, parked in her usual armchair, eyes locked on the TV. Some overacted melodrama, Ann figured, though she wasn't paying much attention. Grace turned her head just slightly, glancing over her shoulder. "Planning on tea?"

"You want some?" Ann asked, voice neutral.

"I'll pass, thanks."

Grace always passed. Tea, coffee, even water. She refused anything Ann offered. A quiet little jab, just enough to draw blood but not cause a scene.

Ann filled the kettle, letting the silence stretch before breaking it herself. "How's the movie? Any good?"

"Oh," Grace said lightly, but with that edge Ann knew too well. "It's a love story. Two very different people. Different backgrounds. Total opposites." She smirked, eyes flicking to Ann before returning to the screen. "But opposites do tend to glue to each other, don't they?"

The words landed like a dart. Ann didn't need a decoder. Grace was talking about her. About how she, a girl from a small, ordinary family in Huntsville, had ended up with her son— Mark Lancaster, the product of British lineage, old money, and pride. Grace never missed a chance to remind Ann that Mark's ancestors arrived in Canada with more than just suitcases. They brought status. Superiority.

"They do sometimes," Ann replied evenly, busying herself with the tea. Grace shifted in her chair, movements sharp, deliberate. She paused the TV and turned fully toward Ann, her voice dripping with mock thoughtfulness. "But they never work properly, these relationships. Not in the long run, right?"

Ann said nothing. What was there to say? Grace didn't expect a response. She just wanted her words to hang in the air. A truth delivered from on high. Ann stirred her tea slowly, the spoon clinking against the cup. Grace was right, of course. It didn't work. It never had. Not for Ann, at least. She took a sip, the warmth doing little to ease the cold truth settling in her heart.

***

Mark Junior and Lily were adorable kids. Ann often marveled at how much they took after her side of the family—Junior with her mother's quiet intensity, Lily with her father's sharp wit. Mark had noticed it, too. And he wasn't thrilled. Once, he'd made an awkward, clumsy comment about "village genes being stronger." The memory still made Ann's skin crawl. Village genes. God, she hated him for saying that. Her great-grandmother had come from a tiny village in Western Ukraine, meeting her great-grandfather, a Scotsman, at Vienna's bustling city market a few years after World War I. Their love story had been improbable and bold. Knowing his family wouldn't approve, Walter McFadden ran away with Halyna, settling in Canada to start a new life. Walter secured royal land on the outskirts of a tiny town called Huntsville, right on the banks of a breathtaking lake. They built a home, raised six children, and carved out a life that became Ann's foundation. Her grandmother, the youngest of their children, was still alive, a living connection to that history.

Ann missed her family fiercely. Sometimes, when she read to Junior and Lily, her mind drifted to Huntsville, where the past never felt far away. Tonight, the book was about ancient times — Indigenous tribes at war, love, adventure, and survival. As she read aloud, she thought of her own childhood. Forest and water, learning to fish, hunt, and navigate the woods. The wilderness had always been her playground.

Mark's snide genes comment burned even more now. He'd never understand what it was like to grow up with roots that deep, with stories that real. She lowered her voice, turning the page. Junior and Lily were already asleep, their faces bathed in the soft glow of the bedside lamp. For a moment, Ann felt a rare wave of calm. Downstairs, the in-laws were likely finishing up their evening ritual of tea and TV. She had no intention of joining them. Mark was still at work. He wouldn't be home until at least eleven. And when he did come home, it would be the same routine—a quickie he'd insist on, followed by snoring in less than two minutes. She hated that, too.

Ann closed the book, kissed both kids on the forehead, and slipped out of the room. Walking toward her bedroom, she felt her life settling over her, heavy, inescapable. Like a thick quilt, she hadn't chosen but couldn't shake off. Village genes, she thought bitterly. If only Mark knew what strength they'd actually given her.

Chapter 2

The table for six was set in the prime spot of the open veranda, offering a sweeping view of the vineyard. Neat rows of vines stretched endlessly, their green tendrils soaking up the golden afternoon sun, disappearing into the distant horizon. Ann sat with a glass of rosé in hand, her gaze drifting over the scenery, half-listening to the conversation at the table.

Honestly, there was nothing worth listening to.

Mark, Anthony, and Julian, all lawyers, all fluent in the art of self-congratulation, droned on about wealth, status, and the symbols that proved it. Investment strategies, property portfolios, the latest benchmarks of affluence.

Across from Ann, Daniela and Jessica nodded at the right moments, their smiles polite but empty. They knew the script. They played their part.

Ann didn't.

Mark stole a few glances at her, his expression tight, each look a silent rebuke: Engage. Smile. Look like you care.

Ann ignored him. Her mind was far from the table, lost somewhere in the clouds, the vines, and the endless questions she kept turning over in her head. Was this her life now? Afternoons spent like this? Polished tables, shallow conversations, pretending to care?

Julian decided to steer conversation back to the wine. "So, ladies, what do you think of the wine tasting?"

Jessica immediately tuned in. "Oh, I loved the Chardonnays." Daniela followed with a nod and an emphatic, "Absolutely! Terrific."

Ann didn't even glance up.

Julian, undeterred, turned his attention directly to her. "What about you, Ann?"

Lifting her eyes to meet Julian's, she spoke calmly. "I guess, for a climate like this, these people put in an unbelievable amount of effort. I do appreciate the working hands. The result is simply amazing."

Her words hung in the air.

The mention of "working hands" landed awkwardly. It wasn't what they had expected — too real, too far removed from their detached, leisurely appraisal of vintages and labels. Julian nodded, forcing a smile, while Daniela and Jessica exchanged uncertain glances. No one openly disagreed, but their silence was telling.

Ann could feel their discomfort and decided to let them sit with it. She rose from her seat, excusing herself with a faint smile.

As she walked away, she felt a tiny ping of satisfaction.

***

When Ann stepped out of the washroom, she saw Anthony heading her way, his eyes scanning for the restroom sign. When he spotted her, he smiled a little too warmly and stopped directly in front of her.

"Hey, Ann," he said, his tone casual but with an undercurrent of something else.

His lusty eyes roamed over her with an intensity that made her uneasy, his gaze unfiltered and brimming with a desire so blatant it felt almost indecent. Ann tensed. She could sense it. He wanted to say something, and whatever it was, it wasn't going to be good.

Then he said it.

"Never seen you this unhappy," he began, his voice low, conspiratorial. "Guess he's doing a lousy job." His eyes lingered on her breasts in a way that made her skin crawl. "I could fix that, you know... if you're into a tiny secret affair."

25

The words hit her like a lightning bolt. It wasn't only the audacity, it was its raw, unfiltered boldness. Direct. Blunt. Disgusting. And coming from one of Mark's so-called friends.

Ann didn't flinch. If anything, she steadied herself, meeting Anthony's gaze head-on.
Then, with a faint, biting smile, she said, "Wow, Anthony, bold move. You must think very highly of yourself and very little of me to even suggest that." Anthony's confident smirk faltered, but Ann wasn't done. Let me make this clear: I'm not the kind of woman who sneaks around with men like you. And frankly, the fact that you'd even approach your friend's wife with this says everything I need to know about you." She paused, letting him squirm under her gaze, then added, "You might want to save this routine for someone with your kind of standards. Better luck next time."

Anthony's smile disappeared, and his face drained of color. "I... I just... I like you. A lot," he stammered, his usual lawyerly composure nowhere to be found.
Ann's eyes didn't leave his. "Well, too bad," she said sharply, her voice like steel. "Because I don't like you." Without another word, she brushed

past him, her shoulder grazing his as she made her way to the veranda door. Anthony stood frozen in place, his confidence shattered. It took him a full ten minutes to recover and rejoin the group, though his face was still flushed when he finally sat down. Ann didn't glance at him once.

But she did glance at Anthony's wife, Daniela, more closely. Poor woman, she thought. You have no idea your husband just offered to sleep with me right under your nose. What a great family life!

Studying her carefully, Ann tried to decode the person in front of her. Daniela was calm, soft-spoken, and noticeably quiet. When Mark spoke, she wouldn't look at him, her gaze deliberately averted, her head dipping slightly as if distancing herself from his words.

Then, Ann noticed how Daniela reacted to Anthony. With her husband, she was different. When he spoke, she turned toward him almost confrontational, as if testing whether his words were even worth listening to. There was something in her eyes, something sharp and simmering. Hatred? Ann wondered. Or just deep, exhausted loathing? She wouldn't be surprised. Daniela probably knew Anthony was sleeping around.

Ann's attention settled on the unusual choker around Daniela's neck. It was striking. Black with gold threads woven through, fastened by an elegant lock-shaped connector with a sizable diamond in the center. Beautiful, sophisticated.

Then their eyes met. For a split second, Daniela held Ann's gaze before it drifted away, settling instead on Mark's hand wrapped around his wine glass. Ann watched as Daniela studied his fingers probably admiring how long and perfectly manicured they were. How typical, Ann thought. A woman checking out a man's hands.

Ann pretended to follow the topic about whether rosé paired better with chicken than red wine. It was all noise to her now, distant and irrelevant. She took a slow sip of her wine. The conversation flowed around her, but Ann, intrigued by her discovery about Anthony's wife, kept a subtle eye on Daniela without drawing attention to herself. Mark was telling some wine joke and Daniela slipped back into quiet compliance, her expression unreadable, her presence almost fading into the background.

Ann turned her gaze to the vineyard, the rows of perfect vines stretching toward the horizon. From a distance, it all looked effortless, untouched. But up close, every branch was bound, every growth controlled, pruned, kept in line. Some things thrived under control. Others just waited for the right moment to break free. Ann took another sip of wine, the crisp taste biting her tongue. She couldn't wait for this party to end.

***

Back in the car, heading back home, Mark decided it was time for one of his lectures.

"Look, Ann," he began, his tone clipped, "I hate to bring this up, but you don't have to make it so obvious that you're not interested in my friends. Sitting there like you're miles away, creating this... absence. Everyone noticed. It didn't play well."

Ann kept her gaze forward, her fingers tightening around the edge of her seat. She wanted to react, to spill every thought she'd been holding back all night, but instead, she said quietly, "I don't care."

Mark's face darkened instantly. "You should care. These are the people I invited. I'm not going to sit by while you ruin my relationships with them."

That did it. Ann turned to face him, her voice rising with a sharp edge. "Oh, right. I forgot. Caring is in my fucking job description."

Mark's hands tensed on the steering wheel. "What's that supposed to mean?" he shot back, glancing at her briefly before turning his attention back to the road.

"It means," Ann said, her words measured but biting, "you expect me to care about the things that are important to you. But when's the last time you even tried to care about what matters to me?"

Mark blinked, thrown off by the challenge. "What are you talking about? What matters to you?" His tone was part defensive, part genuinely clueless. "You've got a great life, you've got two wonderful kids, and we'll buy our own house next year. What could possibly be wrong?"

Ann stared out the window, the passing lights blurring into streaks of gold and white. Finally, she shook her head, her voice barely above a whisper.

"Nothing. Nothing's wrong."

Mark opened his mouth to convince her, to lay out all the reasons she should be happy. But for the first time, the words caught in his throat. A strange hesitation, fleeting but undeniable. He pushed it down, hard, and focused on the road instead. The silence that followed was thick and oppressive, neither of them daring to break it. The rest of the drive passed without a single word uttered, each of them lost in their own thoughts, the distance between them growing with every mile.

***

The next day was Sunday, and Mark always took the kids skating at the arena nearby. It was his only regular routine with them—Sunday mornings from ten to noon, and he preferred to do it alone, without Ann. It felt, to her, like some sort of ransom he paid for his absence during the rest of the week.

Ann hated that routine. It didn't match her idea of what a father should be. Her dad had spent so much time with her growing up, no matter what sport or hobby she'd been into. He'd always been there, cheering her on, showing her she mattered. Mark's two hours on a Sunday felt like a token effort by comparison.

With the kids out of the house, Ann grabbed her jacket, whistled for Spike, and slipped away before Grace could rope her into anything. The day promised to be beautiful, that rare kind of early fall warmth that still carried whispers of summer.

She walked along the lake, Spike trotting happily beside her, his nose busy with the scents of the dog world. Her thoughts wandered, untethered, as she followed the curve of the shoreline.

That's when she saw him again. The stranger.

He was sitting on a rock right at the water's edge, his figure unmistakable even from a distance. His dog wasn't with him this time. He was alone.
Interesting, Ann thought. Looks like an escape from the house. Just like me. Just like me...
She kept walking, slowing only slightly as she passed by. He didn't turn to look at her, his gaze fixed on the horizon. She couldn't see his face, but the line of his back told her more than she expected.

His posture spoke of someone carrying not a physical load, but a heaviness rooted deep in the soul. Shoulders slumped, head slightly bowed, as if life had filled his bag with too many stones, leaving him crushed under a relentless strain he no longer had the strength to resist. Ann hesitated for a second, her steps faltering, but she kept going. Whatever burdens he carried were his alone, just as Ann's own were hers to bear.

But the scene touched her. She felt an inexplicable sense of companionship with the man she didn't know, a shared understanding, even in silence. It seemed clear that he, too, was escaping from the house. She couldn't help but wonder what his reason might be.

Escape usually meant one thing: the atmosphere was unbearable. Ann knew that truth all too well. She'd been living it for the past seven years. Oh, they could have moved out long ago, of course. But Mark had insisted they stay with his parents while he saved for the house he truly wanted. Not just any home, a mansion in a neighborhood that screamed success, where every neighbor was someone worth bragging about.

Ann didn't care much about that kind of life, but anything would have been better than living with her in-laws. She told herself to be patient. Mark claimed that next year, they'd finally be ready to move. The down payment was enormous, well over a million bucks, but Mark was determined. For him, it was another symbol to add to his carefully built image of success.

Ann huffed under her breath, her gaze drifting back to the man on the rock. She noticed a woman walking purposefully toward the man. Ann paused, instinctively sensing the unfolding drama. Pretending Spike was interested in something in the grass, she stopped, letting the dog bury his nose in the world of smells.

The woman approached the man but stopped about ten feet away, her body stiff with tension. She yelled something, her voice sharp and accusing. The man turned to her and replied, his tone too low for Ann to catch. The woman shouted again, louder this time, her gestures agitated, her body language brimming with anger.

Ann felt she should move and leave the scene behind. But her feet refused to cooperate, rooted in the soft grass as if held there by the weight of the confrontation. The exchange escalated quickly, though Ann couldn't make out the words. The woman threw her arms up in a dramatic gesture, one that screamed frustration and finality. A gesture that said everything: I'm done with you.

The man didn't react. He didn't yell back, didn't plead, didn't move. He simply turned his head back toward the horizon. The woman spun on her heel and began walking in Ann's direction, muttering furiously under her breath. As she drew closer, Ann noticed her face was twisted with rage, her eyes narrowed with hatred. She shot Ann a sharp, almost accusatory look as if she knew Ann had done something unforgivable. For a moment, it seemed like she was about to say something but then, she didn't.

Ann recognized her. She'd seen the woman a few times around the neighborhood, though they'd never exchanged more than a polite nod. She must be his wife. Whatever unfolded between them felt immense and unvarnished, stripped down to something painfully real.

Ann felt like an unwelcome, unwilling witness to someone else's family drama. It unsettled her. This was a different kind of conflict, not like hers. This had more emotion, more action, more intensity.
Her own marriage was nothing like that. Hers was silent, British in style: carefully manicured, hidden from public view. She couldn't imagine Mark chasing after her or creating a scene outside. No, their wars were quiet, smoldering affairs where hatred burned slowly but steadily,

and heartache built up like cholesterol clogging arteries. Silent, deadly, inevitable.

This scene by the lake was the complete opposite. It was messy and unfiltered, full of sharp edges and public displays. It was too raw, too demanding, too exposed. What the hell was happening between them? What had driven the wife to follow her husband, to hurl words at him she felt couldn't wait until they were home? Or maybe he wasn't going back home this time.

You never know, Ann thought, a chill running through her. She tugged gently on Spike's leash, turning him off the path and away from the lake. She needed more time. More space. A quiet moment to digest what she'd just seen before she could head back to the house and resume her own, carefully hidden drama.

***

After lunch, when the in-laws retired for their afternoon nap, and Mark claimed he needed to review legal documents for a new case, the kids dragged Ann out of the house for a soccer match at the park. Both Lily and Mark Junior loved playing, and Ann, who had honed her skills during her years in rep soccer back in high school, was more than happy to indulge them. For half an hour, the three of them played with abandon, laughing and shouting as they kicked the ball across the field.

When they were too tired to keep going, they collapsed onto the grass near the goal, the sun warm on their faces.

"Hey, Mom," Lily piped up, turning her head to look at Ann. "Do you think Dad knows how to play?"

"Of course he does," Ann replied with a faint smile.

Lily grinned mischievously. "I'm not so sure. When I told him about my game at school, he asked me what an offside was..."

Ann laughed, shaking her head. "Oh, I see your point. He might not be the best soccer player, but he knows a little."

Lily giggled. "He should play with us sometimes."

"Yes, that's a great idea," Ann said, faking enthusiasm. "But he's too busy, Lily."

Mark Junior sat up, brushing grass off his shirt. "He's always busy except for Sunday skating. Honestly, Mom, I wouldn't want to live like Dad when I grow up. What's fun about it?"

Ann looked at him, her smile fading into something more serious. "Everyone has their own idea of fun, Mark. For your father, law is fun. Work is fun."

"Boring!" Lily exclaimed, leaping to her feet and grabbing the ball. "Shall we play the second half?" she shouted, already running back to the field.

Ann stood. "Sure thing!" she called, grinning as she followed her daughter.

***

Ann closed the book, switched off the lights, and quietly slipped out of the kids' room. The little soccer enthusiasts had barely lasted two pages before drifting off, exhausted from their day. She gently shut the door and made her way to the bedroom.

She could hear the sound of water running in the bathroom as she entered the closet to grab her nightwear. As she unbuttoned her shirt, the bathroom door opened, and a moment later, Mark stepped into the closet.

"Hmm," he said, his voice low. "That's the sight I like to see." His eyes lingered on her body, unapologetically admiring her.

Ann said nothing. She reached for her nightgown, trying to maneuver past him, but Mark stepped closer, wrapping his arms around her from behind and pressing his lips to her neck.

She stiffened.

"What's wrong?" he murmured, his breath warm against her skin.

"Nothing," she replied, her voice calm but distant. "I just need to go to the washroom."

"I don't think so," he whispered.

His hands moved and gripped her shoulders, and Ann felt it—a small but deliberate push downward. A signal.

His breathing grew heavier, his fingers pressing into her skin with increasing urgency. His lips moved along her neck, trailing into her hair. He wanted her on her knees.

She tensed. Resisted.

They froze in a silent battle of wills.

Ann knew, with absolute certainty, that she wasn't going to do it even if he tried to force her. Mark hesitated, torn between two paths: to break her for the first time in their marriage or to wait, to see if she would finally submit.

But he already knew the answer. He could feel it in the tension of her body, the way her muscles coiled, the way her chin lifted, the way her shoulders squared in quiet defiance. She wouldn't.

A dark thought slithered through his mind, whispering that this was the moment. The moment to turn the tide, to reshape their marriage into what it was always meant to be. He could almost see Ann on the floor, her arms wrapped around his ankle, crushed, submitted, defeated. And the choker locked on her beautiful neck. The symbol of possession.

His breath hitched.

And then, just as suddenly, his heart skipped, a familiar, unwelcome tremor. The same way it always did with Ann. And he let go.
"Right," he muttered, stepping back.
Ann slipped out of the closet and into the bathroom, shutting the door behind her. She leaned against the sink for a moment, staring at her reflection in the mirror, before turning on the shower.

When she returned to the bedroom, Mark was sitting up in bed with a book in his hands. She slid under the covers quietly, hoping to end the night in silence, but Mark closed his book and set it on the nightstand.
Do you think I'm blind, Ann? That I don't see the signals you're sending?" he asked, his voice laced with as much venom as he could summon.

Ann froze for a second, then propped herself up on her elbow, her expression blank. "What do you mean?"

Mark looked at her, his jaw tightening. "You're avoiding me, Ann. It's as clear as day."

She sat up fully now, realizing this wouldn't be a short exchange. "What makes you think that?" she asked cautiously.

"Everything," he said, his tone sharp but controlled. "The sex is clearly unwanted on your side. My friends aren't welcome. You can't even pretend to care. And then, ten minutes ago, you tried to..." He was searching for the right word but never found one and added, "You're not interested, Ann. It's obvious."

Ann stayed quiet, her fingers twisting the edge of the blanket. His words struck her, the truth of them hanging in the air. She couldn't argue. He was right.

After a long, heavy pause, she said something she had never said before. Something she didn't even know she was ready to admit.

"You're right, Mark. I'm not interested. Especially in your power games."

The words hung between them, sharp and final.

Mark swallowed hard, his Adam's apple bobbing visibly. For a moment, he looked like he might say something, but no words came.

Ann lay back down, pulling the blanket up to her chin, waiting for him to speak. But the silence stretched on, heavier than anything either of them had ever said.

***

He didn't say a word in the morning. No goodbye, no glance in her direction, just the sound of the door closing as he left for work.

Ann followed her usual routine, got the kids ready, dropped them off at school, and returned home. She made herself a cup of tea and sat at the kitchen table, staring out the window as the steam curled around her face. Grace was nearby, bustling with her preparations for the evening meal. But Ann could feel that icy stare boring into her.

Mark must have said something.

When Ann finished her tea and stood to grab Spike's leash for a walk, Grace finally spoke.

"Admit it," she said, her voice clipped. "You aren't happy here, Ann."

Ann froze. She placed her cup on the counter and turned to face Grace. A long conversation was clearly looming, and there would be no way to avoid it.

"It's... complicated," Ann said, her voice calm but guarded.

Grace crossed her arms, her eyes narrowing slightly. She waited.

Ann hesitated, then sighed. "I don't have a life," she admitted. "This isn't how I imagined things would be. A husband who's home for maybe an hour and a half a day, no one to talk to, no friends, no job." She paused, her throat tightening. "It's tough."

Grace nodded, but it wasn't a nod of understanding. It was the kind of nod that said I knew it all along as if Ann's words were merely a confirmation of a long-held belief.

"Yes," Grace said finally, her tone cold and deliberate. "I've always known you weren't the right fit for Mark. He needed a woman who would embrace the role of a wife, someone who'd love taking care of him, the kids, and the house. Someone who would be his wall, his support."

She paused, her voice dropping to a sharp whisper. "Someone who'd give him a BJ after work and before work. The way I did for my husband. And look where it got me—a safe, happy family. You were never that type."

Ann felt her breath catch, her heart hammering in her chest as Grace turned back to the counter. But Grace wasn't done. Without looking at her, she added, almost casually, "He made a mistake."

The words hit Ann like a physical blow, as if the ground had given way beneath her feet, and she was free-falling straight into hell. Her mother-in-law had just torn into her; worse, she had annihilated her, declaring with brutal clarity that she was the wrong woman for her son, and implying that Mark might be on his way to correcting that mistake.

Ann swallowed hard, forcing herself to remain still, to stay in control. She said nothing, knowing instinctively that anything she might say while drowning in such overwhelming emotions would only come back to haunt her. Instead, she reached for Spike's leash with trembling hands and walked out of the house.

***

Ann's thoughts buzzed like restless bees gassed by a sudden chemical spray, scattering wildly before falling into a dazed silence. Her head spun, and her mouth was dry. It took her a good twenty minutes to steady herself, to let the swirling chaos in her mind settle into something resembling clarity.

So, she thought, Mark had spoken to Grace. Complained, most likely, about her, about the marriage, maybe even about last night, when she turned him down. Or perhaps he hadn't needed to say much at all. Grace could have pieced it together herself, reading Mark's frustration with the precision of a woman who had spent a lifetime mastering the art of understanding men.

Grace had a radar for that kind of thing. She always knew when to act, when to close the door to her husband's study, and lock it behind her. Ann remembered the early days of living in the house, how Grace would disappear into the study with a faint but deliberate click of the lock.

There had never been any obvious sounds, but Ann had understood soon enough what was going on. One afternoon, years ago, Ann had been planting flowers outside under the study window. She glanced up briefly, catching a reflection in the glass. It was faint, but the corner of the window caught just enough of the computer screen for her to recognize what it was. The old man was watching porn. Ann paused, her spade resting in the dirt, a ripple of unease washing over her like she'd stumbled into a corner of her in-laws' personal life that was never meant to be uncovered. A few minutes later, right on cue, Ann noticed Grace's shadow pulling the shutters closed in the study.

Ann connected the dots, recalling the countless times she'd heard Grace's phone beep, watched her glance at the screen, get up, and make her way to the study. Now, years later, Grace had unwittingly confirmed everything Ann had suspected back then.

That was the way Grace chose to run her family, and for some reason, she had decided Ann should follow the same path just as Mark had followed his father's. His father was a selfish, egotistical man who provided but demanded everything be done his way, expecting a woman to serve him without question. But Ann was cut from a different cloth, and it had taken her years to grasp Mark's vision of family life fully. By the time she understood, Mark Junior and Lily were already a part of her world.

Clarity returned, and Ann finally saw Grace's words for what they were. They weren't only meant to sting and label. They also pointed toward an exit, laying the groundwork to end an unhappy marriage. Naturally, for Grace, the focus was solely on her son's happiness and comfort. The kids, Ann, and the inevitable mess of a divorce were just collateral damage. What mattered to Grace was Mark's peace of mind and his orgasms, delivered on schedule.

Ann's thoughts drifted back to the day she moved in. Back then, the in-laws had been kind to her, believing she was the one to make Mark happy. That evening, they were all gathered in the family room, tired but content after a long day of unpacking. The conversation danced around the idea of a happy family life, with Grace leading the discussion. Tipsy from a few glasses of celebratory champagne, she leaned toward Ann, winked, and giggled quietly before whispering, "Empty balls do the trick."

Ann hadn't quite understood it at the time.

Chapter 3

The following week, leading up to Thanksgiving, was spent in near-total silence. Mark stuck to his routine of coming home late and leaving early while Ann busied herself with the kids and housework. They moved around each other like strangers sharing the same space. Their interactions were stripped down to the barest essentials.

The only real exchange came one evening when Ann finally broke the silence.

"I'd like to take the kids to my parents for Thanksgiving," she said. Her tone was calm but firm. "I think it's best for everyone to have a break."

Mark looked at her, his face unreadable, his eyes flickering with a mix of resentment and indifference, though Ann couldn't quite tell which one held the greater weight. His response was just one word.

"Fine."

The kids were bursting with excitement about their trip to Huntsville. To them, it meant pure freedom and adventures in the woods with Grandpa, lazy afternoons by the lake with Uncle

Jack, and endless fun. They didn't even bother asking why Dad wasn't coming along.

By Friday morning, school had been skipped, the luggage packed into Ann's Toyota, and the three of them, plus Spike, hit the road. Three and a half hours later, they were greeted with open arms by Grandma, Grandpa, and Uncle Jack, who the kids absolutely adored. Jack was still single, which meant endless energy for the kids. Ann welcomed the break. Her parents, Scott and Laura, were equally happy to see them all.

"Hey, honey, love to see you home," her dad said, pulling her into a warm, familiar hug before helping unload the luggage. "I made us your favorite Muskoka coffee. Want some outside?"

Ann smiled, "Sure, Dad. Who says no to Muskoka brew?"

Laura, thrilled to see the kids, laid out snacks while Uncle Jack corralled the three of them behind the massive kitchen island. Stories from school, sports, and friends spilled out effortlessly, drawn out by Jack's playful questions and Laura's warm encouragement. The laughter and chatter filled the house, and for a moment, it felt like happiness had descended onto her, wrapping Laura in the joy of having the family together again.

Meanwhile, Ann and Scott had settled into the Muskoka chairs on the dock, steaming coffee mugs in hand.

"I'm so glad you came for Thanksgiving," Scott said, leaning back in his chair. "The weather's unbelievable. I don't think I've ever seen such a warm October."

"Absolutely," Ann replied, taking a sip of her coffee. "Thanks for having us, Dad. You know how much I love Thanksgiving. We're lucky to have it in October, unlike the Americans. It still feels like summer here."

Scott nodded but said nothing for a few seconds, studying her profile as she gazed out at the water. He knew something was wrong the moment she'd stepped out of the car. His little girl was in trouble.

"So, how have you been, Ann?" he asked gently.

Ann turned to him, and for a fleeting moment, Scott thought he saw tiny diamonds of tears glinting in her eyes, catching the sunlight.

"Things have been... strange, Dad," she said quietly. Her voice wavered, but she didn't falter. "I feel like my marriage is coming to an end."

Scott reached over and placed his hand firmly on hers, grounding her. "Whatever happens, honey,

I'm here for you. I'll do anything to make sure you and the kids are okay."

Ann nodded, her lips trembling. She let out a small, choked sob but managed to keep the tears at bay.

Scott didn't press for details or reasons. He knew they didn't matter, not to him, anyway. What mattered was that Ann was ready to share this with him. His daughter needed him, and he felt a quiet resolve settle within himself. He would stand by her, no matter what. She was his blood, his only daughter, and he loved her more than life itself.

***

The day had been fantastic. Jack took the kids out on the lake. Fishing, skipping stones, running wild that was exactly what they needed. Later, after dinner, when the kids were sound asleep, the family gathered in the living room. The fireplace crackled and popped, sending flickers of warm light across the room. Scott poured everyone a glass of red wine, and the conversation flowed with ease—stories about the kids, updates on the neighbors, and snippets of local gossip Ann was eager to hear.

When the local news ran out, Ann felt the silence stretch. She stared into her wine glass, swirling the deep red liquid, then took a slow breath. It was time. Her turn now. She looked up at her dad, her mom, Jack.

"Guys..." Her voice was quieter than she expected. "I've been going through some rough times lately." She swallowed. She almost wanted to laugh at how small those words sounded compared to what she really felt. Rough times. What an understatement.

She pushed forward. "Well... it didn't happen overnight, but I've been unhappy for months. No, years, actually."

There. She'd said it. And it hung in the air, solid and unmoving, like it belonged there all along.

"Mark..." She let out a sharp breath, shaking her head. "Mark lives for work. Hitting the next goal, making the next big move. It makes him happy. Work, money, success, symbols. That's what matters to him. And he thinks it should be enough for me, too. That I should be some happy little wife, some perfect mother, waiting at home while he builds his practice."

Her voice hardened.

"But I can't do it anymore. I can't pretend anymore."

She sat up straighter, her hands gripping the blanket draped over her legs.

"I adore my kids. I'd do everything for them. I wake them up, feed them, dress them, take them to school, soccer, swimming, birthday parties, help them with their homework, read to them, play with them, stay up when they're sick, and comfort them when they cry. I make sure they are safe, loved, and cared for. And I do it alone. Because Mark is never fucking there."

Her mother's lips pressed into a thin line. Jack shifted in his seat, his jaw tightening. Her dad set his glass of wine on the coffee table with a sharp, deliberate thud, with enough force to say what he didn't.

"The only thing keeping me sane is my dog. Can you believe that?" She let out a sharp, humorless laugh. "A fricking dog is my lifeline. He's the only reason I step outside twice a day. Well, not exactly true... It is him and my in-laws who, by the way, never miss a chance to remind me how lucky I am to be Mark's wife. How grateful I should be to live in their house. Can you imagine? I'm thirty-eight and feel like a guest in my own life."

She stopped, suddenly feeling lightheaded. The room was silent except for the crackling of the fire. Three pairs of eyes were fixed on her, absorbing every word, every breath, every ounce of pain she had just poured out. Then, Scott let out a long, slow sigh as if trying to process everything. Jack muttered a single word under his breath - "Bastard." And Laura didn't speak. She only sat there, shaking her head, her eyes filled with quiet sorrow.

Ann paused, looking down at her hands as if searching for the right words. "And then there's the way I'm treated... It's... strange. In their family, a wife is expected to take care of her husband. And I don't just mean cooking or cleaning. It's this unspoken rule that a wife exists to serve. You know what I mean."
She cleared her throat and continued, her tone steadier. "And Mark... he's obsessed with these... status things. Like, we can only have this size of a house, the kids have to go to this school, we must live in this neighborhood, drive only these types of cars, meet these kinds of people. It's like it's all burned into his brain."

Ann gulped down her wine and set the empty glass aside.
Laura finally spoke, her voice soft but steady. "My girl, it aches me to hear this and see how unhappy you are." She tipped her head back and added, "And I can only tell you this: trust me, there's no magic in this world." She gave a small, sad smile. "Apart from Santa, of course. But

things won't just get better on their own, Ann. If you want to change your life, do it. Everyone will be happier."

Ann nodded slowly, her fingers tracing the rim of her empty glass. She turned to her dad.

Scott shook his head, agreeing with Laura. "We'll stand by you, no matter what," he said firmly. "Count on us for anything, from the costs to full-time babysitting. He paused and then added, "And, Ann, I do remember you were always the type to just up and leave when something didn't feel right."

Ann swallowed hard, emotion swelling in her throat. She had known they would support her, but hearing it out loud, so unshakable and certain, still made something deep inside her crack.

Jack leaned back in his chair, arms crossed. Then he looked straight at Ann. "And you never thought—" He hesitated, then went for it.

"You never wondered if he had someone else?"

Ann blinked, caught off guard.

"I guess I never really wanted to know."

"You said Mark is into all this status-driven bullshit, right?" His voice was measured, but there was something sharp underneath.

"I've seen guys like that. They chase prestige, luxury, and the next big thing. I mean, in his world, status often means having a mistress, doesn't it?"

The question hit her like a thunderbolt.

Her mind went blank. She had never, not once, considered that possibility. She had accepted Mark's faithfulness as a given, never questioning his late nights at the office, his weekend business trips to the U.S., or those sudden, urgent Saturday meetings with his partners. Not once had she doubted him. Not once had she allowed herself to think that maybe she should.

"I don't know," Ann said quietly. "I've never had a reason to suspect him of being unfaithful."

The silence that followed was heavier than words. Jack hadn't been asking a question. He was searching for answers, trying to understand why Ann's life had felt so empty, why Mark was always absent. And the more he thought about it, the more it made sense. Men like Mark rarely left obvious clues. They didn't have to. They covered their tracks with one simple, foolproof trick — being too busy. Always working, always unavailable, always somewhere else.

Now, watching Ann's face, he felt a pang of regret. Had he just made things worse? Had he forced her to consider something she had never questioned before?

Jack ran a hand through his hair, suddenly regretting saying anything at all. "Shit. Sorry, sis," he muttered. "I didn't mean to—"

Ann shook her head before he could finish. "I know, Jack. I know. That's okay."

Scott, sensing the shift in energy, decided it was time to steer the conversation elsewhere. He pushed himself up from his chair and clapped his hands together.

"I'm getting another bottle of wine," he announced. "And then we're having Laura's cheesecake. Trust me, it's unbelievable."

Ann let go of a breath she didn't realize she was holding, grateful for the distraction. "Great idea," she said, forcing some lightness back into her voice. "I'll help Mom."

Laura gave her a knowing look and squeezed her hand before leading the way to the kitchen.

Chapter 4

The mood at the Thanksgiving dinner table was far from festive. Grace watched Mark closely, sensing the storm raging beneath his composed exterior. He was angry. Angry at Ann, at himself, at the empty chair that should have been hers. She had dared to skip Thanksgiving in this house. She had taken his children and driven them up north, choosing her family over his. At the time, he had agreed. Now, he hated himself for it.

Grace's disapproval sat between them like an unspoken accusation. Mark could feel it gnawing at him. He knew how she saw him. Weak. And that was unbearable. He had spent his entire life measuring himself against her standards, waiting for her approval, needing her validation.

His father, George, couldn't have cared less. Ann and the kids being away didn't faze him, nor did the fact that Mark might have made a mistake in letting them go. Why should it? George spent years grinding away as a senior partner in one of the country's most prestigious law firms. He had retired with more money than he could ever spend, not that he needed much. A man of simple pleasures, his indulgences boiled down to three things—his finest and most expensive Scotch collection, which he consumed daily with ritualistic devotion, his antique telescope, and his insatiable obsession with sex. George knew there was something wired differently in his brain. It wasn't normal. He knew that. Because how else could a man his age, sixty-eight, still crave it daily? Still need it like oxygen?

He spent hours watching porn, lost in fantasies he had long since stopped questioning. But nothing compared to the real thing, his finest hour, his sacred ritual. The moment when he summoned Grace into his study, watched her lower herself onto her knees and took in the sight of his devoted wife, servicing him like the obedient slut she was.

The conversation at the table lost George's interest quickly. The turkey was half-eaten, the chatter had dissolved into meaningless gossip, and all he could think about was a well-earned glass of Scotch. He mentally sifted through his collection, debating which of his finest, oldest bottles deserved the honor.

Grace and Mark were caught up in talk about one of Mark's friends—some idiot who had just gotten engaged and was currently parading his fiancée around Italy. George tuned it out, pushed back his chair, and headed for the cellar.

As soon as he was out of sight, Grace seized the moment. She lowered her voice.

"So? What do you think? Where's this headed?"

Mark, still chewing on a bite of turkey, met her gaze. He took his time, swallowed, and then answered flatly, "Guess the divorce. She's turning into a gigantic pain in the ass."

Grace nodded, unsurprised. She opened her mouth to say something, but George reappeared, bottle in hand, looking pleased with himself.

"Who wants to try this beauty?" he announced, holding up the Scotch like a trophy.

Mark raised a hand, his mouth still full of turkey stuffing.

George grabbed another glass, poured for both of them, and took a long, satisfied sip. Then, he glanced at Grace and Mark and smirked. "I'll see you soon."

With that, he took the bottle and disappeared into his study. Grace didn't need to ask where he was going or what he was about to do. She already knew. She probably had about half an hour before her phone would beep.

Grace held Mark's gaze, her expression unreadable at first. Then, with quiet certainty, she said, "Well, you're right about that. She was the wrong choice, Mark. I could have told you that from the start."

She took a slow sip of her wine, then added, "She was never going to be the wife you imagined. And let's be honest. You never even had a chance to bend her to your will. She's stronger than you. No match."

Mark swallowed hard. He had known Grace would say that. He had known she would seize this moment to remind him of his failure.
Grace had always been an enigma. A woman trained to obey, but with a quiet, relentless power of her own. She played the part she was given, but Mark had seen the truth early on—she was never just a pawn. She was the one who knew when to kneel and when to strike.

He clenched his jaw, forcing down the resentment clawing at his insides. Because she was right, he was weak. And Grace had known it all along. A memory crashed into him, painful, humiliating. Years ago, after one of his first explosive arguments with Ann, Grace had pulled him aside. Her voice had been calm, patient, almost gentle like a mother teaching a child a simple, necessary lesson.

"Don't leave it like that," she had said. "She needs to learn her place."

He hadn't been sure what she meant. He had nodded, left the room, and done nothing.

And to her greatest disappointment, he hadn't won.

The next morning, she barely looked at him as she poured her coffee. But before leaving the kitchen, she hesitated just long enough to twist the knife.

"Loser."

Mark snapped back to the present. He knew better than to argue with his mother. Deep down, he had always known Ann was stronger than him, but strangely, that had never bothered him. It bothered Grace.

"Divorce is a good way out," he said almost casually.

Grace was clearing the table, swapping plates for dessert. At his words, she looked up, her movements slowing for just a beat.

"You don't say," she murmured.

Mark frowned. "What do you mean?"

She set a plate down with deliberate precision, her eyes locking onto his.

"Mark, if you're serious about heading down that road, you must be prepared. Otherwise, this whole thing could backfire, and you'll be the one on the losing end, my dear." She paused and then added, "You must clean your backyard mess first."

Her words made his stomach clench. And then she gave him that look—the one that had frozen him in place since he was a boy. Cold. Knowing. He almost stopped breathing.

She knew.

The realization hit like ice water down his spine. His mother who had never missed a detail, who saw through him like glass, was telling him, in no uncertain terms, that his secret wasn't a secret at all. But how? How the fuck did she know?

Mark had been sure he had covered his tracks. He had safeguarded everything and played it carefully. No loose ends. And yet, here she was, looking at him like she had known all along.

Grace resumed clearing the table, barely sparing him another glance. But as she walked past, she muttered, almost amused, "I'm your mother, for fuck's sake, Mark. It's my job to know everything."

Mark swallowed hard. He didn't sleep that night.

***

It happened on one unfortunate Saturday morning, three years ago.

Grace had been waiting for this call. Her longtime butcher rang to let her know he had just received a fantastic foie gras delivery, the very one she'd been anticipating for an important dinner she was hosting for George's friends in a week. There was one problem: her car was in the shop, George was off playing squash, and Mark, Ann, and the kids were still lounging in bed, savoring their slow morning.

But Grace wasn't about to wait.

She spotted Mark's car keys on the counter, grabbed them without hesitation, and headed downtown. The trip was quick, and soon she was back in the town's parking lot, her precious cargo secured. A fortune spent, but well worth it.

She placed the frozen container carefully into a bag, then reached for a tissue to wipe her hands. She opened the glove compartment, rummaging through the usual odds and ends, manuals, receipts, a stray pen. No tissues.

But something else caught her eye.

A sleek, elegant black box. Jewelry. Definitely jewelry. Grace stilled, her fingers hovering over it. For a long moment, she simply stared. Then, slowly, she picked it up.

She immediately assumed it was for Ann. Mark must have hidden the gift in his car, waiting for the right moment to surprise her.

But curiosity burned through her, hot and insistent. Carefully, Grace lifted the lid.

Her heart kicked against her ribs.

Inside was a choker, stunningly crafted, made of elegant black material woven with delicate gold threads. At its center sat a symbolic lock, adorned with at least a carat diamond.

Grace took it out of the box, running her fingers over the intricate design. Beautiful.

Then she turned it over.

On the underside of the lock, barely visible, was a small engraving. A single letter.

'M'.

A slow smile curled her lips. Well, well... He finally did it. He finally made a slave out of her.

The choker was unmistakable, a mark of ownership, a Master's claim.

"Well done, my boy," she murmured, chuckling to herself. That's the way to do it…

She, of all people, would know. Her own collection was extensive. Some pieces were discreet enough for public wear, others were meant only for private submission. These days, though, George didn't bother with such elegance. When he felt his Grace the Slut needed

65

correction, he preferred a simple, unrelenting dog collar and a leash.

Weeks passed. Then months. But Ann never wore the choker. Nothing about her demeanor changed, and Grace quickly realized that Mark had never given it to her. Still working up to it, she had thought at the time. She had held out hope, imagining the day Ann would finally wear it. That would be a victory. The victory.

And then, nearly three years later, it happened but not in the way Grace had expected.

Mark and Ann were heading to Niagara wine country with friends, and Mark's colleague, Anthony, stopped by for coffee on the way. He had his wife, Daniela, with him.

Grace was in the kitchen when she saw their car pull into the driveway. She stepped outside to greet them, polite and poised as always. She knew Anthony, but Daniela was new to her.

And the moment she saw her, it was like being struck by lightning. Not because Daniela was beautiful. But because of the goddamn choker around her neck.

For a split second, Grace went speechless. Then, as if all the puzzle pieces had been scattered in front of her, the truth clicked into place.

66

Mark had failed to break Ann. So he had simply found someone else. His friend's wife.

Grace felt trouble brewing. This was dangerous. Reckless. But she recovered instantly, slipping into her usual flawless performance, welcoming them inside with effortless charm.

As they sat down for coffee, Grace was glued to Daniela, watching, studying. The way she avoided Mark's eyes. The way she listened when he spoke, hanging on his words. The way her head dipped ever so slightly, a quiet, instinctive bow. Grace knew. She also knew that no one else did.

Grace was cutting into the mango cake, a true masterpiece to accompany their coffee, when Daniela stepped into the kitchen.

"Can I make some more coffee for Mark and Anthony?" she asked.

Grace gestured toward the machine. "Sure. Just press the button."

Daniela fidgeted for a moment, pressing the buttons until the machine hummed to life. As the rich aroma of coffee filled the kitchen, Grace spoke, her voice light, almost casual.

"That's a beautiful choker, Daniela."

Daniela glanced down, touching the delicate lock at her throat. "Thank you, Grace," she said with a small smile. "I bought it in New York three years ago as a reminder of my master's degree at NYU. Kind of locked myself to that city."

Grace nodded, but her mind was elsewhere. "Expensive toy", she said and smiled, but in her thoughts, the words were different. Oh, sure. NYU. A Master's. What a perfectly neat little lie for your husband, sweetie. And a smart one, considering the lock on that choker. Grace knew exactly what it meant. Daniela didn't belong to New York. She belonged to Mark. And by extension, she belonged to her. Grace let her gaze roam over Daniela's body, taking in every curve and every delicate feature —imagining, just for a moment, what she might do with it one day.

***

As Mark casually mentioned divorce, Grace felt two things at once—satisfaction that he was finally making the right decision and deep concern for what could happen if his extracurricular activities ever came to light. If that happened, it wouldn't just be messy. It would be war. Ann wouldn't go quietly.
In Grace's mind, Mark didn't need that kind of problem, but she also knew there was no

undoing it now. It was already there, sitting beneath the surface like a sleeping volcano, ready to erupt when least expected.

She had told him to fix it.

And from the look in his eyes, she knew he understood exactly what she meant. So she let him sit with it. Let him think. But mentally, she made a note that if he didn't handle it soon, she would because some messes didn't clean themselves.

Chapter 5

Their goodbye was filled with tight embraces, lingering looks, and a silence heavier than words. Scott, Laura, and Jack stood outside, watching as Ann and the kids loaded into the car, holding onto every last moment. Laura's heart sank. She would miss them terribly. Scott, though steady on the outside, was sick with worry, knowing his daughter was returning to a life she hated. And Jack was boiling inside. He loved his sister. Always had. And the thought of her trapped in that marriage with that man made his blood simmer with rage.

Mark, the polished, self-important prick who had never once made an effort with Jack, never even pretended to see him as an equal. No, Mark had always been too high up to acknowledge the villagers. Jack had sensed it from the start, and he had despised him ever since.

As Ann's car disappeared down the driveway, Laura turned and headed inside, unwilling to stand in the emptiness it left behind. But Scott and Jack remained.

They stood side by side in silence, staring at the empty road. Scott placed a firm hand on his son's shoulder. "Jack, your sister's in trouble." His voice was low, certain. "The divorce is coming. And trust me, it's going to be messy. That guy will make sure she gets nothing, or as little as possible. And there'll be a fight over the kids."

Jack's jaw tightened. He already knew.

Scott gave his shoulder a squeeze. "Why don't you take a closer look at him? See if your gut is right. Maybe he does have a secret."

Jack turned to face his father. He didn't speak, just nodded once. Sharp, deliberate nod. But Scott saw it all in his eyes. Determination. Stealth. A quiet, unshakable promise to protect his sister at any cost. Scott slapped his son's back and walked inside. Jack didn't move. He stood there, taking in the crisp autumn air, the damp earth, the scent of fallen leaves. His gaze stretched over the horizon, past the trees, past the lake. Time to bring her home, he thought, looking southeast, toward where Ann was heading.

***

Mark's coffee was getting cold. His friend was already thirty minutes late.

When he finally spotted Steve walking into the coffee shop, he raised a hand, signaling him over. "Hey, buddy, awfully sorry!" Steve said, sliding into the seat across from him. "Couldn't leave the location until my partner showed up. We've been doing some surveillance on a house."

"Yeah, no problem," Mark said. "I get it."

Steve, his old university roommate, had taken a different path after law school. He worked for his uncle's private security firm, a business that thrived on hiring people with legal backgrounds. They didn't just need people who knew the law. They needed people who knew how to bend it.

That's exactly why Mark had called him.

Divorces were ugly, and Steve's clients, wealthy husbands and wives, were always collecting dirt on each other. Mark wasn't about to walk into this blind. If Ann decided to play clever, he needed an ace up his sleeve.

Steve took a sip of his coffee. "So, what's up, buddy?"

Mark leaned in slightly. "This stays between us."

"Sure thing," Steve said easily.

Mark exhaled, his voice flat with resolve. "I want out. Divorce. But I don't expect her to go quietly, and I sure as hell don't want to spend more than I have to. She could take as much as half. I am not willing to give her half."

Steve nodded, already shifting into work mode.

"So," Mark licked his dry lips, "I want to know how to do this right."

"All right." Steve set his cup down. "Tell me, do you suspect she has any secrets? Anything hidden?"

Mark shook his head. "Nothing. She's clean."

Steve considered that for a moment. "In that case, some guys hire a Casanova."

Mark raised an eyebrow.

"A guy who's good with women," Steve explained. "His job is to seduce her. Ours is to discreetly record it. Boom. Adultery. You become the wronged husband, the victim of a cheating wife. Judges love that. Makes things easier."

Mark nodded slowly. "It's not a bad idea. But I don't think it would work on Ann. She's too fucking straightforward, black and white, you know?"

"Right." Steve thought for a second. "You know what? Let's start simple. I'll get you three trackers and an app. One for her car, two for her favorite purses. Install them, and we'll monitor her movements for a few weeks. See her patterns, see if there's anything to work with. Then we decide."

Mark smirked. "Deal. Thanks, buddy."

"No problem." Steve leaned back, already switching gears. "Anyway, tell me, how's work?"

Their conversation shifted to Mark's cases, then to Steve's latest assignments. They wrapped up thirty minutes later, settled the bill, and walked out.

**

Ann and the kids arrived home late Tuesday afternoon. Mark had flown to Boston for a two-day working trip. Grace and George had left to visit friends and were expected to be back late. The house was empty. Just the way Ann liked it.

The kids settled in with a movie downstairs while she unpacked and started dinner. By all accounts, their trip had been fantastic. Junior and Lily hadn't stopped talking about Huntsville, their voices animated, reliving every adventure. No wonder Mark and his parents had made themselves scarce. They would've hated listening to it.

Ann smirked bitterly.
What a great fucking life I've built for myself.
The exact kind of life millions of people were trapped in, bound by kids and responsibilities, weighed down by resentment, silently enduring the presence of a once-significant other who had become little more than a stranger across the dinner table.
And now, she was one of them. But not for long.

This fake family, this fake marriage, this fake life—it all had to go. She would find a way out.

She walked to the window. Outside, the wind had picked up, rattling the branches. The street was dark, and the sky hung heavy, threatening rain.

How many more times will I stand here, looking at this view before I leave for good? Not many, she promised herself.

Then she saw him. The man with the dog. The stranger. He was walking slowly past the house, his dog on the leash, his head slightly bowed. And then, as if sensing something, he lifted his gaze toward the dark window. He couldn't possibly see her in the unlit room, yet for a brief moment, he hesitated.

And then, just barely, his head moved. A subtle nod. A quiet acknowledgment. A signal. Or maybe just a hello.

Ann stood there, watching until he disappeared down the street. Then she turned away and went to read to the kids.

***

"And they lived happily ever after."

Ann finished the story and closed the book. The bedroom was dark and still, the soft rhythm of her children's breathing filling the quiet. She rose from the chair, ready to leave, when a small voice stopped her.

"Mom, I need to confess something."

Ann turned. Lily's voice was barely above a whisper.

"What is it, sweetie?" Ann whispered back, careful not to wake Mark Junior.

Lily shifted under her blanket, turning toward her. "Mom, I love Grandpa and Grandma. And Uncle Jack. But I don't like Grandma and Grandpa here." She hesitated, then asked, "Am I a bad person?"

A wave of emotion washed over Ann. A mix of right and wrong. The quiet pleasure of knowing her daughter loved her parents, but also the undeniable confirmation that this marriage was a life she needed to leave.

Ann sat on the edge of the bed and brushed a strand of hair from Lily's forehead. "That doesn't make you a bad person, sweetheart. Think about it. Scott, Laura, and Uncle Jack don't get to see you often, so every visit is special. Grace and George see you every day."

Lily fidgeted with the corner of her blanket. "Yeah, but they don't even notice me."

Ann swallowed. There was no easy answer to that.

"Don't worry, sweetie," she said softly.

Then, from the other bed, a quiet voice whispered,

"Mom... why don't we live in Huntsville?"

***

By the time George and Grace left the party, rain had begun to fall. It was already late, close to midnight, and on top of that, they had an hour's drive home. The downpour would add at least twenty extra minutes. George was fuming. Not just because of the rain, but because of Grace. She had signed them up for this damn party without properly checking the guest list, and as a result, he'd been forced to spend the evening in the same room as the man he despised most.

Walter.

His old friend from university. The one who had outpaced him in every possible way. Walter, who had built a legal empire while George had merely worked for one. Walter, who wasn't even thinking about retirement while George had been nudged into it, settling for a life of expensive Scotch and duller victories. And worst of all, Walter, who had shown up with his third wife, thirty years younger, grinning like the smug bastard he was, slapping her ass in front of everyone just to make a point.

George hated that.

Though, if he was being honest, when it came to ass-slapping, he could give Walter a ten-second head start and still win. But that wasn't the point.

The point was, he had told Grace, expressly told her, that he never wanted to see that idiot again. And yet, here they were.

The car was silent for twenty full minutes before George finally spoke. His voice was measured but edged with ice.

"I'm not happy with you, Grace."

She remained still, eyes fixed ahead.

"I'm thinking," he continued, after a deliberate pause, "that you should be punished tonight for this oversight."

Grace lowered her head. She had made a mistake. A careless, foolish mistake. And mistakes had consequences. She knew better than to argue. Speaking now would only make it worse. She simply had to wait for his decision. It came five minutes later, his tone so even, so casual, it could have been mistaken for small talk. "This time, your misstep qualifies as punishment in the basement room, Grace."

She inhaled sharply. Her gaze flickered, almost involuntarily, to George's belt, thick, cowboy-style, lined with small metal spikes. She could already feel them. Tearing into her flesh.

***

Panting, his hand aching, George finally stopped. Grace lay trembling, silently crying through her ball gag, her body shaking but her posture rigid, absorbing the pain as she always did.
George tossed the belt aside with a huff. "You're not allowed in the Master bedroom tonight."
With that, he unbuckled the cuffs from her wrists and ankles and left without another word.
The basement room was always locked, always hidden. It was George's domain. No one else apart from Grace in the house had ever set foot inside. George was the only one with a key; the door was cleverly concealed behind a heavy mirror that slid open on command. It was soundproof, smartly designed, and stocked with everything he needed to ensure Grace the Slut stayed in line.

Grace moved slowly, wincing as she dressed, her body screaming from the welts searing into her skin. She deserved it. She made her way to the guest bedroom in the basement and checked the time. Almost 4 a.m.

Collapsing onto the couch, she pulled a blanket over herself, but sleep never came. Instead, she burned. Not with anger. Not with resentment.

With need.

But she wasn't allowed in the Master bedroom to service His Highness. Not tonight.

Frustrated, she threw off the blanket and went to make coffee. As the machine hummed, she noticed the rain had stopped. The house was still, steeped in silence. She needed air.

Taking her favorite cup and slipping into a warm overcoat, she stepped outside. The streets were dark, empty, and quiet, their world still untouched by the morning rush. The wind carried the last traces of rain, warmer now, almost soothing against her skin.

Grace took a slow sip of coffee, inhaled deeply, and started walking.

Turning back onto her street, Grace passed the first two houses when she heard the low hum of an approaching car. Headlights swung into view, cutting through the damp air.

One of the neighbors, she thought, instinctively stepping under the thick oak tree, pressing herself against its trunk, blending into the shadows.

But the car didn't continue down the street. It stopped right in front of her, pulling into the driveway just twenty feet away. Grace stilled, cautiously shifting her position to make sure she was fully hidden behind the trunk.

At that very moment, the front door of the house creaked open, and warm light flickered on. A woman appeared in the doorway, barely dressed. Melanie. The neighbor.

Grace watched as Melanie leaned in, kissing the man standing in the threshold. Probably her husband leaving for an early flight. Maybe an Uber to the airport, she reasoned. The man kissed her back, lingering, then turned and walked toward the waiting car.

That's when Grace saw his face. Her stomach lurched. She almost gasped out loud but caught herself just in time.

Anthony. Mark's friend. Mark's colleague.

Casually strolling out of Melanie's house like it was routine. He slipped into the car, and moments later, it disappeared down the street. The front door shut, the lights went dark, and the house fell silent again.

Grace remained frozen, stunned, listening to the quiet hum of her own pulse. It was minutes before she finally stepped out from behind the tree and walked home, her mind spinning. Back in the kitchen, she poured herself another cup of coffee, staring out the window as she pieced it all together.

Mark said he left for Boston. With Anthony. And yet, Anthony had just left Melanie's house. The same Melanie whose husband was very much in town. So where the fuck was Mark?

Daniela.

Grace paced slowly, sipping her coffee, the pieces clicking into place.
Anthony must have fed Daniela some excuse, some reason why he'd be gone for the night. Daniela, in turn, must have let Mark know. And Mark, conveniently, had told Ann and Grace he was out of town. Grace's eyes flicked toward the

counter, where a sliver of moonlight caught the rim of her coffee cup.

He's with her. The choker flashed in her mind. Her son's slave. A slow, knowing smile curled at the corner of her lips. This thing with Anthony could be a fucking gold mine.

***

It had rained through the night, and by morning, the air was unusually warm and damp, the ground slick with yesterday's downpour.

Ann returned from dropping the kids at school and muttered a quick hello to Grace, who was in the kitchen, but didn't slow down long enough to invite conversation. Before her mother-in-law could say a word, she was out the door with Spike.

Last night, her in-laws had come home after she was already asleep. Mark had been out of town on business. She suspected he'd planned the trip on purpose. His way of punishing her for skipping Thanksgiving. Fine. Let him. She was used to it. Right now, all she wanted was fresh air, space to think, and to be anywhere but that haunted house.

She turned onto the trail, half-expecting it to be too muddy but still willing to check. It wasn't bad. The air was crisp, and the earth smelled fresh, washed clean by the rain. Just as she passed the small lake where the path curved right, she nearly collided with him. The man with the dog. The stranger. Spike tugged toward him, and his dog did the same. Clearly, the two animals had been waiting for an introduction. The man stopped.

And for the first time, it was not just a nod, not just a polite lip movement imitating the word 'morning'. This time, he actually spoke.

"Hello," he said simply, smiling.

Ann hesitated for only a second before returning it. "Hi."

Then, to her surprise, he added, "I'm sorry for my window-peeping last night."

"What?" Ann blinked.

He chuckled. "I saw you at the window. I almost said hi. I guess I've gotten so used to seeing you all the time that when I spotted you, I instinctively wanted to say hello."

Ann let out a short, awkward laugh, but something about the way he said it, so casual, made her stomach tighten. Window-peeping? Had he been joking, or was there a sliver of truth buried beneath his smirk? She thought back, suddenly uneasy. A few nights ago, lying in bed, she had the distinct feeling of being watched. Not a noise, not a shadow. Just a prickle at the base of her neck, a deep, instinctual certainty that eyes had been on her. She had dismissed it as paranoia.

"Oh." Ann finally managed a smile. "Never mind. I was just... well, looking outside. Checking if it had rained."

"It had," he nodded. "Started just as I was driving back..." He trailed off, his expression shifting like he had just said something he shouldn't have.

Ann caught it immediately. "Back? Back where?"

A tired, almost sorrowful smile flickered across his face. "Yeah... well. I... no, I just meant the rain caught me while I was driving."

Ann didn't press, but something about the way he deflected made her curious.

"Anyway," he said, offering his hand, "I'm Daniel."

She took it. "Ann."

His face lit up. "I knew it! I knew your name would be Ann."

She raised an eyebrow. "That's... odd. How would you know?"

"I didn't." He grinned. "I just imagined you'd be an Ann. Or an Anna."

"Hmmm." She narrowed her eyes playfully. "Sounds like you've been spying on me."

Daniel's expression changed, his eyes suddenly gleaming like a kid about to share a secret. And then, in the most unexpected turn of events, he said something that left Ann completely stunned. "Well... in a way, I have."

Her stomach tensed slightly, but before she could react, he added, "I'm writing a book, to be honest. And, well... you've been—" He hesitated before finishing, "—my inspiration."
"Me?" Ann's brows shot up.

Daniel nodded. "It's true. But first, let me apologize because, well... I might have taken some creative liberties." He gave a small, almost sheepish smile. "I don't really know you, Ann. But I've seen you around, always walking the same trail, always with your dog. And at some point, I started imagining a story... and, without realizing it, I made you the protagonist."

"Wow," Ann said, then paused, studying him. "How does it end?"
Daniel smiled. That same deep, effortless smile. But for a moment, his eyes turned serious.
"That's the thing," he said, shaking his head. "I don't think it does."

Then, running a hand over the back of his neck, he added, 'If you're curious, I'll tell you all about it.'

Ann looked at him, still trying to process it all.

Here was this man—someone she had always known yet never actually met. And now, just like that, he stops, says hello, and she learns that she is the heroine of his novel, or whatever it was he was writing. That's weird, she thought. Could this just be some elaborate excuse to talk to me?

Unlikely.

They had been crossing paths for at least three years, and not once had he ever initiated contact. Until now.

"Well," she said, still intrigued, "I'd love to hear about it. Have you finished your walk? Because I've got another thirty minutes."

"I've got all the time in the world," he said simply.

And with that, they fell into step, walking together down the trail.

"So, how exactly did I end up as the star of your book?" Ann asked, a teasing note in her voice. Then, before he could answer, she added with a small smirk, "Never been a muse before."

Daniel met her gaze and smiled. "I don't know. It just happened." He sighed, his voice turning reflective. "I had a business fallout, a bad one. It terrified me. No matter what I did, I couldn't fix it. I spent hours staring out the window, thinking. And then, I saw you."

Ann arched an eyebrow. "You've seen me on the trails before."

"Yes," he admitted. "But from the window, it was different. I noticed things. The way you walked, always at the same time, always alone. You looked... lost. Or maybe I just imagined it. Maybe I was projecting. But something about you made me wonder. Who is she? What's her story? And then, before I knew it, the idea turned into a novel."

He hesitated before adding, "I even named you Anna and it turns out I was only one letter away from the truth."

Ann let out a small, thoughtful laugh. "That's interesting." A beat of silence passed before she asked, "What happened to your business?"

Daniel tapped his fingers against his thigh, stalling for a second. "Long story short? Google killed it. I had two platforms that connected students with math tutors. They ran well for nearly a decade, but then search algorithms changed, traffic disappeared, and no matter what

I did, I couldn't bring it back. The revenue tanked to almost nothing."

Ann let out a slow breath. "That's brutal."

He nodded. "Yeah. But it forced me to slow down. And that gave me time to write."

She smiled faintly. "Funny how life throws curveballs that sometimes turn into opportunities." Then, curiosity flickered in her eyes.

"And what's the book about? What exactly am I, well, your Anna, in this story?"

Daniel glanced at her. He paused. "Well, Anna is trapped in an unhappy marriage. One day, she accidentally discovers her husband is having an affair. And then—" He stopped, as if weighing whether to say it.

Ann tilted her head. "Then what?" she prompted.

He sighed, almost reluctant. "The woman he's having an affair with falls from an office building," Daniel said.

Ann's eyes widened. "Oh my God. Did I just kill her?"

PART TWO: THE STRANGER

Chapter 6

"Damn it!" Daniel slammed the door hard enough to rattle the frame and stormed out of the house, not sure if he was actually leaving or escaping. Betty, his black lab, sensed the tension. She didn't tug at the leash, just trailed beside him, casting wary glances his way as if checking whether his frustration had anything to do with her. It didn't. Daniel loved his dog. Betty understood him perfectly. His wife, on the other hand, spoke a language he no longer cared to translate. Whatever she shouted back at him was lost to the closing door, but he didn't need to hear the words to know they were sharp enough to cut.

The last six months had been unbearable, and no matter how much he tried to ignore it, he knew their marriage was on the verge of collapse. He was still holding on mostly out of habit, the drag of shared years, and the complicated mess of their move to Canada. Melanie, his wife, had insisted on it. She had landed a well-paid job with a Polish-Canadian company running a network of grocery stores in the GTA and made sure Daniel followed. Not that he had wanted to move. Not that he had fought it, either.

He walked along the narrow trail in the neighborhood, inhaling the scent of early autumn, trying to shake off the last argument. God, he thought. Why does she make my life so fucking miserable? It felt deliberate as if she was doing it on purpose. Or worse, with purpose.

The constant fighting had reached a breaking point, and they both knew the resolution was just around the corner. What rattled him most was the nagging feeling that Melanie was working for it, pushing him, maneuvering him toward one inevitable outcome—him leaving. And maybe she'd get exactly what she wanted.

The truth was, Daniel never thought his second marriage would end like this. He had stepped into it with hope, with certainty, believing he was building something real. Now, all he felt was regret. Deep down, he acknowledged his mistake. Two, actually. First, he let lust masquerade as love, mistaking sex for affection. Second, he failed to see Melanie for what she truly was—calculating and relentless. Her charm, her beauty, her body. They weren't gifts;

they were weapons, and he had been too blind to recognize he was the target.

His thoughts drifted back to home. Real home. The place he had left, only to end up here, in a foreign country, unhappy, and ruined.
Eleven years younger than him, Melanie had come into his life just as his first marriage crumbled. She had been unstoppable in her pursuit, and he had let himself be swept up in it. But through their decade together, one thing had become clear—she never wanted children.

Daniel already had a son, born from the kind of reckless, all-consuming love that only a teenage heart can produce. His high school sweetheart had married him at nineteen, and their son had been the center of his world. Now, that boy was a grown man with his own life.
Melanie, now at thirty-seven, was nearing the point where motherhood was no longer a debate. And somewhere along the way, the idea of having a child with her had simply... evaporated, just like everything else between them.

They were both from Poland, born and raised in Warsaw, in similar middle-class families. But their paths had unfolded differently.

By twenty, Daniel had a baby boy and the crushing responsibility that came with him. He hustled through various jobs, climbed his way up, and eventually built a successful online business selling math tutoring services worldwide. Daniel launched several online platforms that connected students with tutors, charging a small subscription fee for access. He focused on math specifically. Its universal nature made it the perfect bridge between students and teachers across different countries, languages, and time zones. It was smart. Scalable. And for a while, it was thriving. The money started flowing. Not extravagant wealth, but a solid half a million a year.

By the time his son left for university, his marriage had quietly run its course. He and his ex-wife had waited patiently for that milestone, then, with mutual relief, bolted in opposite directions. She found comfort in the arms of a Swedish architect she'd met at a conference. Daniel, meanwhile, embraced his well-earned freedom. Their relationship remained amicable. No grudges, no unfinished business, just two people who had done their time and moved on. His freedom, however, barely lasted six months.

Then came Melanie.

He was 38. She was 27. And the sex was phenomenal. It felt like love. Or at least, something close enough. So he dove in, convinced he was building something new, something lasting. His business was thriving, early retirement was on the table, and for a while, it all made sense.

Seven years later, Melanie got the job offer in Canada. She was ecstatic. She spun it as an exciting new chapter, something they had to do. Daniel wasn't exactly thrilled, but his English was near perfect, and Canada sounded like an adventure. Besides, as soon as Melanie received the offer, their sex life skyrocketed—a detail that didn't go unnoticed.

So they moved.

The first year wasn't bad. Melanie put effort into their relationship, and Daniel, feeling the momentum, poured most of his savings into an expensive property. Settling down was fun. Expensive, but fun. Candlelit dinners and expensive wines in their new house. Weekend trips to Niagara. Skiing in Québec. Lobsters in Nova Scotia. It wasn't paradise, exactly. But for a while, it was close.

***

Daniel kept walking, his thoughts tangled, his pace steady. Betty, usually eager to sniff every tree and investigate every rustling leaf, was unusually quiet. She simply trotted beside him, matching his steps with quiet devotion, doing her job, loyally staying close to her favorite person in the world.

His thoughts began to settle, the fog in his mind lifting. At least he had this trail, this quiet time with his dog. A small escape from the relentless attacks at home. Nothing he did seemed to be enough.
"I fucking hate seeing you sitting behind that desk all day," Melanie would snap, each time aiming to cut deeper.

It had all started two years ago, when his business had nearly collapsed. His websites lost traffic overnight, crushed by Google's ever-changing algorithms. He tried everything — poured money into web traffic, tested different strategies, chased every lead he could find. Nothing worked. What had once been a thriving business had slowly dwindled to scraps.

By then, most of his savings had already been sunk into their move to Canada. And now, he was staring into the abyss of financial ruin. He had a safety net, some money stashed away, but he figured it would barely last two years. And then what? He needed something new. And fast.

But his resources were limited, and the idea of gambling what little he had left on another venture terrified him.

Melanie, on the other hand, seemed to have been waiting for his downfall. The candlelit dinners stopped. The sex disappeared. The arguments became endless. Daniel cursed the moment he agreed to move to Canada. It had brought nothing but disaster.

Then, after months of struggle, his hard work finally paid off, just a little. He managed to salvage parts of the business, enough to keep it afloat. But overall, it had shrunk to a fraction of what it once was. Instead of pulling in half a million a year, he was now scraping by on a measly sixty thousand. Still, it covered the bills.

The only reason he wasn't drowning completely was the house. They had bought it outright, no mortgage, no looming debt. That was both a blessing and a curse. A blessing because at least he wasn't chained to monthly payments. A curse because, thanks to Melanie's taste and insistence on a prestigious neighborhood, the purchase had devoured most of his life savings. And now, with his income barely a whisper of what it used to be, there was no way to rebuild what he had lost.

***

The trail curved around a small lake where geese bickered and chattered, their voices carrying over the still water. Even Betty, melancholic as she was today, perked up at the sound. This place, this quiet stretch of nature, was the only thing about Canada that soothed Daniel. At the house, everything was a battlefield. Regret clung to him like a second skin, a constant reminder that moving here had been a mistake. But the crisp autumn air, the explosion of colors in the trees, the way the warmth of the sun still lingered despite the season shifting, this was his escape. A fragile, temporary relief.

Then, he saw her. Finally.

She was walking fast along the trail, heading in his direction. Her dog, ugly but undeniably enthusiastic, was busy checking every possible corner for something worth investigating. She made his day every time he saw her.

Daniel didn't know her name. He'd never spoken to her. But he knew her. He had watched her enough times to recognize her habits, her patterns. She was stunning, blonde, tall, effortlessly elegant in a way that wasn't about looks alone. There was something about the way she moved, the quiet confidence she carried. It wasn't beauty that made Daniel's heart stutter when he saw her. It was the freedom she projected. The quiet, unshakable strength.

That was what drew him in. That was what made him want to know more.

And, in a way, he had been getting to know her without ever exchanging a single word.

It had started months ago.

Back then, with his business floundering and every attempt at recovery failing, Daniel had found himself with an unfamiliar companion: free time. His hired external SEO team had delivered the final, brutal verdict: if he wanted to regain his lost traffic and income, he'd need to pump at least $30,000 a month into marketing. Money he didn't have.

Panic set in. Then depression.

Daniel spent hours in his study, staring out the window, lost in thought. Watching the world move while he felt stuck.

That's when he really saw her.

Of course, he'd noticed her before, everyone in the neighborhood had. But this time, he paid attention. She had a routine. A purpose. Always walking her dog at the same time, always alone, always deep in thought. And the more he watched, the more certain he became that she didn't belong here. Or maybe she simply didn't want to belong. And just like that, Daniel started imagining. Who was she? What was her life like? Where had she come from? What was she thinking as she walked these same trails, day after day, lost in her own world?

Days blurred into weeks, weeks into months, and strangely enough, Daniel found himself writing a book. Not a business plan, not a recovery strategy, but a real book. It started as a way to untangle his thoughts, a quiet rebellion against the life that had backed him into a corner. But soon, it became something more. A confession. A plea. A story that was his and yet, somehow, not his at all. In his mind, he called it A Stranger I Fell in Love With. And while the book carried the weight of his own regrets, his own unraveling, the heart of it belonged to her, the Blonde. He imagined her trapped, suffocating in an unhappy marriage, bound by expectations she couldn't escape. Desperate to break free. Just like him.

Just like him.

***

As she was about to pass him, he did what had become his quiet routine—he glanced at her with those soft, deep eyes, nodded, and offered the faintest of smiles, as if acknowledging their shared affliction: unhappiness. To his surprise, the Blonde smiled back. Or at least, he thought she did. Her lips moved, just slightly, an attempt at something, recognition, understanding, maybe even hope. A break in the pattern. Something had changed, but Daniel didn't know what. His heart skipped a beat, but he kept walking. He wasn't about to crash into her life, dragging his mountain of problems behind him.

When he got home, Melanie was already at work. The silence was a relief. Daniel fed Betty, poured fresh water into her bowl, and headed upstairs. He already knew what he'd find—the bedroom, as always, would be a mess. He hated it. He hated the chaos of it, the carelessness. He needed to make the bed, not for her, not even for order but just for the small illusion of comfort.

Melanie's clothes were scattered as usual. Some on the bed, others on the floor. Like she had unraveled herself and left the remains behind. He gathered them up, tossing them back into the closet.

That's when he saw it.

On the shelf was an open Intimissimi paper wrapper. Branded. Expensive. Deliberate. A few delicate pieces of underwear still had their tags attached. New, he realized.

He picked one up. Sexy as hell. Another, even sexier, lace stitched in all the right places, openings designed for easy access.

Hmm. Was she trying? Was she thinking about fixing things?

Then he saw the tag on the floor.

Same brand, same style. Which meant she had already picked one to wear for work.

Daniel felt a small, sharp pinch where his heart was. Not pain, not yet. Just a hint of something waiting to be acknowledged.

He shook it off. Overthinking. He was still burned from the argument this morning. Exhaling, he left the closet, made the bed, brewed another coffee, and opened his laptop. He checked his sales report. It was still shit, but at least steady enough to cover what needed covering. Finally, he opened his Word document, pages upon pages of a world that wasn't this one. He breathed out and entered the only place that still felt like a future.

Daniel scanned through the pages. There was the Blonde's life laid bare before him. The life he had imagined. The life he had created. A thought ran through his mind, quick and insistent, like a nagging fly as he re-read the lines. What if everything I imagined was true? He let out a tired smile, but beneath it, something made his skin crawl. Because sometimes, he wasn't sure if he was just writing a story or pulling back the curtain on something he wasn't supposed to see.

Chapter 7

Melanie was on her way to an Italian restaurant for lunch, feeling alive, radiant, beautiful again. Unlike at home. Unlike with Daniel.

Her marriage was ending, and she felt no sadness over it. She had used it fully, squeezed every last drop, and now it was time to move on. Ten fruitful years, she thought. But now, the fruit was overripe, just on the cusp of decay.

Ten years ago, she had set her sights on a promising entrepreneur, divorced, successful, handsome, and far too trusting. His smart little online business made great money, enough to fund a lifestyle she could almost call luxurious. And best of all? He was easy.

When they first started dating, she was the goddess of sex. She gave him everything he wanted before he even had to ask. Within three months, he was completely hooked. He suggested moving in, and she made sure he did it properly by buying a flashy new condo in the center of Warsaw.

Then, the real fun began. Breakfasts in Paris. Shopping in Milan. Skiing in Switzerland. Summers in Greece.

It was almost the life she wanted.

But soon enough, she realized the truth. Daniel was comfortable but not wealthy. His business was decent but not the kind that would land her in Soho's elite circles or tucked away in a sunlit Manhattan loft. She pushed him to scale it, to think bigger. But he either couldn't or wouldn't. A wasted opportunity.

Years passed, and then came the offer.

Melanie had always been good at what she did. A strong HR manager for an international pharmaceutical company, fluent in English, German, and conversational Spanish. But her biggest asset was Polish. A Canadian company with deep Polish roots, owners of a rapidly growing grocery store chain in the GTA, needed an HR lead who could navigate both cultures. Most of their employees were Polish and Ukrainian immigrants. She was the perfect candidate. And Canada was her perfect next move. Not for the job, though. She didn't give a fuck about the job. That was just the ticket in. A stepping stone. A means to an end.

Melanie had a better plan than working for some grocery chain. She needed Daniel to fund her new life, to take everything he had worked for, everything he had saved, and lay it at her feet.

She slipped out of her old skin, mundane, exhausted, fading. And she put on a new one. Flashy. Sexy. Irresistible. Again.

Daniel bought it. And, just as she planned, he bought everything else—the house, the new life, the cars, the entire setup.

Now, she had drained him completely.

Just as she had regularly drained his balls, working hard to get exactly what she wanted.

And when it was all over, Melanie knew she'd walk away with at least a million and a half in her pocket.

A fair price for ten years well spent.

***

A couple of months ago, Melanie sat through yet another dull management meeting with representatives from a law firm they were about to hire. It was the usual corporate drudgery, except for one significant detail. The man sitting across from her. Handsome. Self-assured. And with those lust-heavy eyes, the kind she recognized instantly. Could be my next trampoline, she thought. That's what she called them. The men who propelled her to the next stage of her life.

His name was Anthony Miller.

She gave him a few deliberately slow, well-timed glances. And just like that, he responded. After the meeting, he lingered. Just long enough. As she stepped into the hallway, he caught up to her, his voice low behind her ear.

"Hey. Fancy a coffee?"

"Now?" she asked, turning to face him.

"The meeting's over," he said with a knowing smirk.

She held his gaze, let a small smile play on her lips, and said, "I'm married."

"So am I." He made a slight gesture with his hand—And? When has that ever stopped anyone?

The coffee ended up being served scalding hot—on the white sheets of a nearby Marriott.

The sex was wild. Intense. Melanie gave it everything. Since then, they'd been fucking at least three times a week.

***

"It's delicious," Melanie murmured, purposefully licking the curve of her dessert spoon before flashing Anthony a knowing smile. He caught the meaning instantly. "Oh, I definitely didn't plan on missing that," he said, voice low. "And I want it in the back of my car."

She set her spoon down, her expression turning all business. "Deal."

Anthony laughed. "What a girl."

Melanie leaned back, tilting her head slightly. "By the way," she said, casually shifting gears. "Looks like I'm just days away from living alone, darling."

His eyebrows lifted, amused. "Really?"

She nodded. "Which means way more flexibility. Enough of these hotels. I want you for the whole night."

Anthony smiled. He had stumbled onto a goldmine. This Polish beauty was an absolute machine in bed and effortless out of it. No clinginess, no jealous outbursts, no awkward questions about his wife. She never even mentioned her. Fucking paradise, he thought. They finished lunch, walked to the parking lot, and within minutes, he was sprawled across the back seat of his car, eyes closed, as Melanie worked her magic with those full, sinful lips.

Chapter 8

Editing was a struggle for Daniel. He hated doing it on a laptop. The screen made his eyes ache. The words felt different, somehow less real. Paper was better. He needed to see the pages, mark them up with a pencil, let the words exist in the physical world before they made their way back into the Word document.

He printed a few chapters and settled in, the quiet work wrapping around him like a cocoon. It felt like stepping into another life. The characters weren't just names on a page anymore. They were people he knew. At times, they felt so real he caught himself talking to them, arguing with them, filling in details of their stories that never even made it to the manuscript.

The process was slow but strangely fulfilling. Daniel didn't actually know why he was doing it. Deep down, he had hoped the book might bring him some money. But maybe it was just a hobby. Or perhaps it was something more—an urge to pour his thoughts onto the page, to search for answers he couldn't find any other way. A chance to live through someone else, even if only for a little while.

Under the table, Betty snored softly, lost in whatever dream world dogs visited. Daniel glanced out the window. Twilight was settling in. Soon, he expected to see her, The Blonde, passing by with her dog. Her evening walks were always short, unlike the longer morning ones. He knew why. She had kids. She was busy in the evenings. He also knew she lived with her husband and his parents who actually owned the property. He met them not long after he and Melanie moved in. George and Grace.

Grace was the first to catch his attention. He often saw her tending to the front yard, meticulously trimming bushes or pulling weeds as if her life depended on it. She had the energy of someone who needed to keep busy. Daniel, always polite, had made a habit of nodding or offering a quick hello as he passed. She always responded. But never with a smile. Grace had a way of looking at people that made them feel transparent, like she was searching for something beneath their skin. When Daniel passed her in the driveway, she held his gaze a second too long. Not a glance. An assessment.

His thoughts drifted back to today's morning, the moment The Blonde had smiled at him. Not just smiled. Hesitated. For a split second, she had looked at him differently. Daniel couldn't explain why, but he felt it. He'd seen her on that trail more times than he could count. With anyone else, there would have been at least a polite hello, maybe even a small conversation about the dogs. But not with her. She was different. She struck him as someone who desperately avoided people. No small talk, no friendly dog-owner routine, no complaints about irresponsible neighbors leaving poop on the sidewalk. She never lingered. She never belonged. And Daniel made the only logical assumption—she hated this place. She lived here, but she wasn't part of it.

"Me too," he thought. "But my story's different. I'm an immigrant. She's not."

Step by step, Daniel decoded The Blonde. Step by step, he turned his observations into words, his theories into pages. Nothing escaped his eye.

Not even the small detail that she was the one taking the kids to play soccer in the park. Her husband, he figured, was always busy.

***

Daniel barely had time to save his document before the front door slammed shut. Melanie was home. He blew out a breath, running a hand down his face. The contrast between fiction and reality bothered him. One minute, he was crafting a chilling twist—an office affair turned deadly, a body crashing onto the pavement below. The next, he was back in his own tangled mess, where the betrayals were quieter but just as lethal.

Footsteps clicked against the floor. He could already tell by the rhythm that she was in a mood. Betty, curled up at his feet, lifted her head but didn't move.

Daniel glanced at his screen. Suicide? Not so fast, he had typed. He smirked bitterly. Real life was never that simple, either.

He heard her heels click past his study, then—
"You're still writing that book?"
She didn't even look up from her phone.
"You do realize Amazon isn't some lottery where you just hit it big eventually, right?"
Daniel released a slow meditating breath, resisting the urge to react. Just as he was about to respond, she cut in again.
"What's it even about, anyway?"
He scratched the back of his head, weighing his options. Engage in an actual conversation about the book? Or let it slide?
Better to let it slide.

"It's just about my business journey," he said. "Nothing interesting."

Melanie snorted. "Then why are you writing it?" She finally looked up. "Why don't you just get a real job?"

The words landed like a cheap shot to the gut. He wanted to say I worked my ass off for everything we have. He wanted to say you're living off my work, and you know it. He wanted to say screw you, Melanie. But instead, he swallowed the anger and let it dissolve into silence. She was still his wife, and despite everything, he often wondered — was there a way to fix this? Could he salvage what was left, or had the foundation already crumbled beyond repair?

"I made dinner," he finally said. "Chicken parmigiana. Red or white?"

He heard her rifling through the closet, the sound of fabric rustling. He knew she'd heard him.

A pause.

"White."

Daniel nodded to himself and headed downstairs to serve his wife a meal.

Dinner was quiet. No major arguments, no biting remarks. Daniel figured she was too tired to pick a fight. As he cleared the plates and poured them each another glass of wine, he remembered the Intimissimi package he'd spotted in the closet earlier.

"I saw those absolutely breathtaking panties in the closet," he said, swirling his wine. "I'd love to see them on you."

She shot him a look.

For a split second, he caught something in her eyes—a flicker of hostility, maybe even contempt. Or worse. But it was so brief, so fleeting, that he wasn't sure if he imagined it.

Then, her expression shifted. A pause. A hesitation. And finally, a smile.

"Yeah," she said lightly. "They're cute."

Before he could say anything else, she tilted her head and asked, out of nowhere—

"How are the sales?"

The abrupt shift threw him.

Daniel hesitated, then answered. "Better today. Traffic is growing. Slowly, but growing."

Melanie's smile deepened, turning playful. "That's good news."

A beat of silence.

Then she smirked. "So... your cooking was inspired by those panties, huh?"

"Sort of," he admitted, grinning.

She took a slow sip of wine, watching him over the rim of her glass. Then, setting it down, she leaned in slightly.

"Right," she murmured. "Then why don't you show me how much you missed me?"

As Daniel buried his head between her thighs, Melanie idly scrolled through her iPhone, checking her messages, her lips curving around a thought she almost whispered aloud.

They're all trampolines. Some are used. Some are new.

***

All hell broke loose Sunday morning.

Melanie stormed into the bathroom while Daniel was shaving and slammed a stack of printed pages onto the floor.

"Business life story, huh?" she spat. "Fuck you, Daniel! You think I'm stupid?"

Daniel barely had time to react before she went off like a grenade.

"You're chasing that blonde girl across the street! Dreaming about her! You have no fucking shame doing this to me!" She jabbed a finger toward the window, toward her house. "It's crystal fucking clear, Daniel! You never loved me. You don't love me. You're obsessed with some other woman!"

"Come on, Melanie!" Daniel turned to face her, razor still in hand. "What are you even talking

about? It's a book. A fantasy. An imaginary story. Are you nuts?"
"Fantasy?" She let out a sharp, humorless laugh. "Bullshit. It's clear as fucking day! You want her. Not me."

Daniel's mouth opened, then closed. Melanie shook her head in disbelief.
"You don't even know her!" she threw at him.
"Exactly!" he shot back. "Exactly, Melanie!"
She took a step closer, her eyes narrowing.
"Or do you?" she hissed.

Daniel felt his stomach drop.
"You do know her, don't you?" Her voice was venom now, low and dangerous. "Did you fuck her?"
He threw his towel in the sink. "Melanie, stop right now! What the hell are you talking about?" His voice was rising. "That's insane. I don't even know her name!"
She spun on her heels.
"I don't believe you, Daniel," she said, her voice ice-cold. "You're a fucking traitor. You killed our marriage."

Daniel just stood there. Stunned. Disoriented. Like he had just walked into a scene from a movie he didn't remember auditioning for. Without another word, he shoved past her, stalked downstairs, and slammed the front door behind him. He needed air. He needed out. Without thinking, he started walking down the street, toward the lake.

When the door slammed behind him, Melanie smiled.

What an idiot.

He had just handed her an ace, freed her from the long, drawn-out arguments she would've had to endure to make his life miserable. Instead, he had done the work for her, shortened the path, made it easy.

But she wasn't done. Not yet. This needed a final act, a perfectly executed ending. A scene that would drive the last nail into the coffin of their marriage. She would play it flawlessly — the devastated wife, deceived and discarded, wronged by her husband's sick obsession with another woman.

Well, well. Perfect.

She gave him ten minutes, then grabbed her coat and stepped outside. She knew exactly where to find him.

***

Daniel couldn't believe what had just happened. Melanie had read a few pages and detonated like a land mine. It caught him completely off guard. She had never been the jealous type, not even in situations that would've actually warranted it. And now, over this? A book? A fictional story?

He made his way to his favorite spot by the lake and sat on the rock, staring at the water. His mind, which had been scrambled by the argument, finally started piecing things together. He saw it now, the bigger picture.

This wasn't an overreaction. It was staged. A performance. And a dramatic one at that. Why?

His mind drifted back to the first page of his novel, a paragraph so deeply engraved in his brain he could recite it in his sleep:

"Have you ever thought you'd fall in love with a stranger? I haven't. But it happened. I see her every day through the window of my study, walking her ugly dog. I meet her on the trail, again and again, for months. I have never spoken to her, but I know I am in love."

Melanie had read that. And without stopping to think, without considering that it was fiction, she had snapped. But Melanie wasn't stupid. She wasn't the type to lose her mind over words on a page, which meant she was doing it on purpose. To push him. To force his hand. To end this.

His mind flicked back to the expensive lingerie hidden in the closet. That wasn't for me, Daniel thought. The sudden shift in her moods. The way she'd been dressing differently, texting more, staying out later.

A strange calm settled over him, final and irreversible like the autumn leaves drifting down to cover the rocks beneath his feet.
This was it. The end. And maybe that was exactly what he needed.

Out of the corner of his eye, Daniel spotted a familiar figure emerging from the trail, moving toward the lake. The Blonde.
What a coincidence, he thought, though something about it didn't feel like coincidence at all. As if life itself was staging a moment, handing him an answer he hadn't even formulated yet.
He didn't turn as she walked past, keeping his gaze on the water, but then, sharp, slicing through the quiet, came a voice behind him, in Polish.

"I am fucking done with you, Daniel. Look at this! The moment you show up, here she is!"

He turned.

Melanie stood there, playing the role of the wronged wife with theatrical perfection. Her eyes were wild, chest was rising and falling with practiced fury. He could almost admire the effort.

Daniel took a deep breath, steady. "I knew you'd do this, Melanie. I expected as much." He met her gaze. "I'll move out today. Don't worry about that."

A bitter, humorless laugh escaped her lips. "Fuck you, Daniel." A flick of her hand, a final act of dismissal.

Then, instead of leaving, she turned, marching straight toward the Blonde.

Daniel tensed.

The Blonde had stopped some distance away, her dog nosing at the damp ground. She hadn't heard everything, but something had made her hesitate. Her body language said it all—she was debating whether to leave or stay, caught in the pull of an unfolding moment she didn't understand yet.

Melanie kept walking, her steps deliberate, fueled by whatever scene she was about to unleash. Daniel braced for it. But it never came. Melanie walked past and disappeared between the houses, leaving nothing behind but the aftershock of her presence. He had no way of knowing if Melanie had muttered something to the Blonde as she passed. Daniel let out a slow breath and turned back to the lake. That's it, then. The end of something that had never been love. His mind drifted to the practical. Where would he go? A motel, probably. The only thing he knew for sure now that it had to be dog-friendly. Betty was coming with him.

***

The Thanksgiving weekend was finally over, and Daniel was relieved. For the first time, he had spent it completely alone, just him and Betty, in a motel room with nothing on the Thanksgiving table but a takeout burger, a can of Canada Dry, and his laptop.

The first week after leaving Melanie, he couldn't bring himself to work. His mind kept cycling through the images of his life: the tiny apartments he and his first wife had lived in, the long nights spent hustling to build something from nothing, the thrill of his first real paycheck, and then the moment he crossed into real wealth. He had worked tirelessly, always moving forward, always reaching for more. And in the process, he had missed things.

He knew he hadn't been the perfect husband the first time around. They had grown up together, built a life from scratch, but when they finally became the people they were meant to be, they realized they needed different things. Well, she had realized it first. Daniel, left to his own nature, would have dragged it out, reluctant to face the inevitable. But she had been decisive, and in the end, he knew she had been right.

Then came Melanie. His greatest mistake. The one who had taken everything he had worked for and drained it dry. Soon, whatever was left would be cut in half, and if he was lucky, he'd walk away with just enough to go back to his home country, buy a small house deep in the woods, and spend the rest of his days writing.

What he couldn't let go of were the walks with Betty. Every day, he drove back to the neighborhood where he used to live, walking the familiar trails. He never got too close to the house, never risked running into Melanie, but he couldn't stay away from the paths he knew so well.

The reason, of course, was the Blonde.

Daniel didn't want to miss seeing her. She had become his quiet obsession, his unspoken muse, the fire that kept his book alive. He wasn't ready to let go of that.

The day after Thanksgiving, he took his usual route, but as he walked back toward his car, the evening skies were threatening rain. A shortcut would take him down his street right past his old house. He hadn't planned on passing by, but with the storm rolling in, staying dry seemed more important than avoiding the chance of Melanie spotting him. As he approached George and Grace's house, something in the upstairs window caught his eye — a shadow shifting in the dark. Instinctively, Daniel turned his head, his breath hitching slightly. He couldn't see her clearly, just a silhouette, but somehow, he knew. It was her. Without thinking, he almost nodded. His usual, automatic greeting whenever they crossed paths on the trail. But at the last moment, he stopped himself and kept walking. The encounter put him on edge. She was a magnet, and no matter how much he tried to rationalize it, he was being drawn in.
He needed to talk to her. It was time.

***

The trail was damp, the air crisp with the scent of rain-soaked earth. Daniel welcomed the solitude of his morning walk, the quiet rhythm of his steps, the presence of Betty by his side. These walks had become his sanctuary, the one place where his thoughts could untangle themselves. Then, just as he curved past the small lake, she appeared.

The Blonde.

Daniel loosened his grip on Betty's leash, just slightly, just enough. He had always kept her close when passing the Blonde, but this time, he let her lead. Spike lunged forward, eager, and Betty responded in kind. The dogs had been waiting for this moment. And, if he was being honest, so had he.

Daniel stopped. His usual nod wouldn't do this time.
"Hello," he said simply, smiling.
She hesitated for only a fraction of a second before returning the smile. "Hi."

And then, without fully thinking it through, he added, "I'm sorry for my window-peeping last night."

He saw her blink, caught off guard. "What?"

He chuckled, "I saw you at the window. I almost said hi. I guess I've gotten so used to seeing you all the time that when I spotted you, I instinctively wanted to say hello."

"Oh." She smiled, seemingly unbothered. "Never mind. I was just... well, looking outside. Checking if it had rained."

"It had," he nodded, before catching himself. "Started just as I was driving back..."

Shit.

He saw the flicker of curiosity cross her face. "Back? Back where?"

Daniel forced a tired smile, trying to smooth over the slip. "Yeah... well. I...no, I just meant the rain caught me while I was driving."

He knew she didn't quite buy it, but she let it go. "Anyway," he said, extending a hand, "I'm Daniel."

She took it. "Ann."

The moment he heard it, his face lit up. He had been right.

"I knew it! I knew your name would be Ann."

She raised an eyebrow, amused but wary. "That's... odd. How would you know?"

"I didn't." He grinned. "I just imagined you'd be an Ann. Or an Anna."

"Hmmm." She narrowed her eyes playfully. "Sounds like you've been spying on me."

Daniel hesitated for just a second. Then, without overthinking, he told her the truth or at least part of it.

"Well... in a way, I have."

He caught it, the brief hesitation, the way her gaze sharpened for just a second, as if something unspoken had passed between them. A flicker of a thought she hadn't decided whether to entertain or dismiss. Before she could settle on either, he rushed to clarify.

"I'm writing a book, to be honest. And, well... you've been—" He paused for a beat before finishing, "—my inspiration."

"Me?" Her brows shot up.

Daniel nodded. "It's true. But first, let me apologize because, well... I might have taken some creative liberties." He offered a small, almost sheepish smile. "I don't really know you, Ann. But I've seen you around, always walking the same trail, always with your dog. And at some point, I started imagining a story... and, without realizing it, I made you the protagonist."

She studied him carefully. He braced himself for skepticism, for laughter, for dismissal. Instead, she said, "Wow," then paused. "How does it end?"

Daniel smiled, that same deep, effortless smile. But for a moment, his eyes turned serious.

"That's the thing," he said, shaking his head. "I don't think it does."

Then, running a hand over the back of his neck, he added, "If you're curious, I'll tell you all about it."

She watched him, still processing it all. He could almost see the gears turning in her mind, debating whether or not to humor this stranger who had, apparently, turned her into a fictional character.

"Well," she finally said, "I'd love to hear about it. Have you finished your walk? Because I've got another thirty minutes."

"I've got all the time in the world," he said simply.

And just like that, they fell into step, walking together down the trail.

"So, how exactly did I end up as the star of your book?" Ann asked, a teasing note in her voice. Then, before he could answer, she added with a small smirk, "Never been a muse before."

Daniel met her gaze and smiled. "I don't know. It just happened." He sighed, his voice turning reflective. "I had a business fallout, a bad one. It terrified me. No matter what I did, I couldn't fix it. I spent hours staring out the window, thinking. And then, I saw you."

Ann arched an eyebrow. "You've seen me on the trails before."

"Yes," he admitted. "But from the window, it was different. I noticed things. The way you walked, always at the same time, always alone. You looked... lost. Or maybe I just imagined it. Maybe I was projecting. But something about you made me wonder. Who is she? What's her story? And then, before I knew it, the idea turned into a novel."

He hesitated before adding, "I even named you Anna and it turns out I was only one letter away from the truth."

Ann let out a small, thoughtful laugh. "That's interesting." A beat of silence passed before she asked, "What happened to your business?"

Daniel tapped his fingers against his thigh, stalling for a second. "Long story short? Google killed it. I had two platforms that connected students with math tutors. They ran well for nearly a decade, but then search algorithms changed, traffic disappeared, and no matter what I did, I couldn't bring it back. The revenue tanked to almost nothing."

Ann let out a slow breath. "That's brutal."

He nodded. "Yeah. But it forced me to slow down. And that gave me time to write."

She smiled faintly. "Funny how life throws curveballs that sometimes turn into opportunities." Then, curiosity flickered in her eyes. "And what's the book about? What exactly am I, well, your Anna, in this story?"

Daniel glanced at her. He paused. "Well, Anna is trapped in an unhappy marriage. One day, she accidentally discovers her husband is having an affair. And then—" He stopped, as if weighing whether to say it.

Ann tilted her head. "Then what?" she prompted.

He sighed, almost reluctant. "The woman he's having an affair with falls from an office building," Daniel said.

Ann's eyes widened. "Oh my God. Did I just kill her?"

He chuckled. "That's the mystery. No one knows if she jumped... or if she was pushed."

She gave a slow nod, considering it. "Damn. That's intense."

They walked in silence for a while, the crisp crunch of leaves beneath their feet the only sound. Then, Ann glanced at him.

"Would you let me read it?" she asked. "I mean, whatever's ready?"

Daniel looked at her, surprised. "You actually want to?"

"Of course," she said, laughing lightly. "Since I'm the heart of the story, I'd love to know where this is going."

A slow smile spread across his lips. "There's a coffee shop not far from here. The Coffee Master. Do you know it?"

Ann nodded.

"How about we meet there tomorrow? Same time?"

She studied him for a moment, then shook her head, amused. "Deal."

As they walked apart, a thought lingered at the back of her mind. She wasn't sure why, but she suddenly wanted to know how Daniel's story ended.

PART THREE: THE FALL

Chapter 9

Detective Julia Ricci sat in her car, parked along the driveway, the harsh glow of police lights flashing across her windshield. Yellow tape crisscrossed the property like a twisted gift wrap, sealing off yet another crime scene. It was the third time in two days she had come back to this house, the site of a double homicide. A man and a woman, killed in their sleep by a lethal dose of opioids administered directly into their bloodstream. Two identical injection sites and not a single needle in sight. No struggle, no forced entry. Just the two people lying side by side, as if death had arrived like a lullaby.

Julia rested her forehead against the glass, watching her breath fog up the window as she thought about the case. At first, the pieces had fallen into place too easily.

It had all started with the Fall.

Downtown Toronto, early morning. The city waking up, traffic lights changing, coffee cups steaming, elevator doors dinging open. And then, routine shattered. A body. A woman. Falling from the sky, limbs slack, hitting the roof of a parked car with the kind of sickening finality that made strangers gasp and clutch their chests.

The woman had jumped or so it seemed. Happens all the time. When the police arrived, a small crowd had already gathered, necks craned, phones recording, whispers spreading through the early commuters. Julia had seen dozens of suicides. This one had felt different. At first, no one connected the fall to anything more. Not until the husband who happened to be a high profile lawyer working in the same building, went missing. His office untouched, his phone ringing into oblivion. No signs of him anywhere. A ghost or a killer? No one knew where he was.

Two days later, they had their answer. The call came. Not from the city. Not from the office. From here. From this house in the suburbs. Quiet, expensive neighborhood. The kind of home where nothing ever happens. The 911 dispatcher had barely finished taking the call before police were en route.

They found the husband in bed. Lifeless. Next to a woman who wasn't his wife. No defensive wounds. No overturned furniture. No signs of panic. A single needle mark on each arm.

Julia had walked through the crime scene twice, waiting for that gut feeling to kick in, the one that told her something was off. And it had.

On paper, the case was textbook. A love triangle unraveling at the seams. The betrayed wife discovers the affair. The husband, arrogant, careless, thinking he's untouchable. The lover, collateral damage. A woman scorned. Two quick injections in the dead of night. Then, drowning in guilt, the wife steps off a high-rise balcony.

It was clean. Logical. The kind of case that made perfect sense. Too perfect. If Julia had seen just the bodies, she might have bought it. If she had seen just the fall, she might have believed it. But the two together? Something was wrong. In Julia's mind, these two events tangled the deck, shuffling the obvious into something far more calculated.

Julia frowned, reaching into the glove compartment and pulling out the smooth wooden beads. She ran them through her fingers, one by one, each movement deliberate, seeking the rhythm that always helped her think. Truth hid in patterns, in timing, in the space between what was seen and what was meant to be seen. Bead after bead, the case unraveled in her mind.

A man, lifeless in bed. A woman beside him. A husband. A lover. A perfect scandal. And the wife, the one who should have been the killer? She had jumped. How convenient.

Julia pushed open the car door and stepped out, the cold night air biting at her skin. She lifted the yellow police tape, ducking beneath it as she approached the front door. The Yale lock blinked its waiting light. She punched in the code. A quiet whir, a soft click. The door swung open. Darkness greeted her. She flicked the switch. Overhead lights buzzed to life, casting long shadows across the living room. The silence in the house felt thick, undisturbed, untouched, as if the walls themselves were holding secrets.
She lowered herself into a chair, exhaling slowly, and opened the case file. Pages of reports, photos, witness statements. She flipped through them one by one, letting the details settle, waiting for something, anything, to speak to her.

The missing lawyer's body was discovered alongside his presumed lover, Melanie Nowak, both of them dead. The discovery was made by none other than Melanie's husband, Daniel Nowak, who hadn't been living at home but in a nearby motel. He had been contacted by her employer after she failed to show up for work and remained unreachable. Concerned, he drove to the house, walked inside, and found them. Then he called the police. Now, Daniel Nowak was in custody. Not because they had a solid case, but because his fingerprints were all over the house. That alone wouldn't hold him for longer than 24 hours, and Julia knew it. He had lived there. Of course his prints would be everywhere.

When the bodies were discovered, a solid theory quickly emerged: Daniela Miller, the scorned wife, had killed her husband, Anthony Miller, and his lover, Melanie Nowak, in their bed before taking her own life by jumping from the office balcony.

Julia wasn't convinced Daniel Nowak was innocent, but in a few hours, she'd have no choice but to let him go. He had a motive. He had the means. He knew the lock code. He was smart, capable. And yet, something about this case refused to fall into place. That's why she was here again, staring at the crime scene, trying to piece together what was missing. If Daniela had planned to kill them both and then jump, why had she done it so cleanly? No traces, no forced entry, except for one small but significant detail. According to Daniel, when he arrived at the house, the front door's Nest camera had been deliberately blocked with a piece of double-sided tape. A simple trick, but an important one. Daniela, if she was the killer, must have known the Yale lock code. How?

Julia went back outside, opened the door and examined the entrance. To the right of the front door, a short wall extended out, leading to the garage. If someone approached from that angle, they could have easily reached out with a stick, taped over the Nest lens, and blinded the camera. Once that was done, all they needed was the entry code. The Nest system had recorded perfectly until 4:13 AM. Then, nothing. The dead zone. The perfect hour. When people were in their deepest sleep. Especially after a night of sex.

Then, Julia knew, the lab had confirmed that some kind of sleeping gas had been used before the opioids were injected. That meant preparation. That meant cold-blooded strategy and a precise knowledge of chemicals. It didn't align with the usual statistics of jealousy-driven murders. Those were messy, fueled by raw emotion. This had none of that. It was pure. Clean. Calculated. Julia shivered. She stepped back inside and roamed around the house, checking her notes.

There was something else. Daniela Miller. The security footage from the office building showed her arriving at 9:28 AM on the same morning her husband had been murdered. Julia had analyzed that footage over and over, but one thing refused to let her rest. Daniela had been wearing a choker when she stormed into the building. It was clearly visible on the recording. Not a delicate necklace—bold, black and gold. Heavy and expensive. A statement piece. Unmistakable. But when her body was removed from the scene by the medical examiner, it was gone. Not torn. Not snapped. Just... missing. As if someone had taken it. As if it mattered. No one had touched the body, not according to the security footage. Not according to the witnesses. Not until the police arrived. The evidence bag from the scene held everything Daniela had on her that day. A bracelet. Earrings. A purse. But not the choker. Where was it? Who took it? Was it sentimental? A signature? A message? Or just something too damning to leave behind?

Julia ran a hand over the file's cover, fingers tapping rhythmically. The case had seemed so simple. Too simple. But simple cases don't have missing jewelry. They don't involve sleeping gas. And they sure as hell aren't this perfectly executed. Someone had planned this. Carefully. And that's what made her stomach twist.

Three weeks earlier.

Mark was in his office when the tracking app sent a ping. A red dot blinked on the map, moving beyond the five-mile radius he had set around the house.

His dear wife had left the zone. He zoomed in. Park Land Motel. Mark's pulse spiked. His wife, in a motel, in the middle of the day?

He sat frozen for a moment, staring at the screen, then grabbed his coat and bolted. The drive took him thirty-five minutes, his fingers drumming against the wheel the whole way.

When he pulled into the parking lot, he parked two spaces down from Ann's car and waited. Seven minutes later, she walked out. With a dog. Mark's eyes narrowed. A black lab trotted alongside her as she crossed the lot, heading toward the small park behind the motel. Mark frowned, gripping the steering wheel so hard his knuckles turned white. What the hell is this?

Twenty minutes later, she returned, handed the leash to someone inside, and then came back out, alone this time, walking toward her car.

Mark couldn't sit still any longer. He rolled down his window.

"Hey, Ann!"

She froze mid-step, her hand on the car door. When she turned, the shock on her face was unmistakable.

"What are you doing here, Mark?"

He got out of his car, closing the distance between them in a few strides.

"That's exactly what I was going to ask you, Ann," he said, his voice dripping with venom. "Walking other people's dogs to make some extra cash?"

Her eyes narrowed. "Don't be a smartass, Mark."

"Then what exactly are you doing here?"

"I was helping a friend," she snapped. "He's sick. And by the way, he's our neighbor. Not that you'd know, since you don't notice anyone outside your own reflection."

Mark ignored the jab. His mind was already spinning. A neighbor?

"How did you find me here?" she asked.

He hadn't prepared for that. There was a split-second hesitation, but he recovered.

"Saw your car from the road," he lied smoothly. "I was driving back from a client meeting."

She stared at him. Suspicious.

"There's no point spying on me, Mark."

"Actually, there is," he shot back. "And I have every reason to believe you're having an affair."

Ann let out a short, humorless laugh. "Are you really this desperate for a spectacle, Mark?

But Mark wasn't listening. He was already moving.

Straight to the motel room door she had just walked out of. He knocked, loud. A few seconds later, the door swung open, and there he was, the neighbor. A familiar face, yet so insignificant Mark couldn't even recall his name. Except he looked like absolute shit—red eyes, a tissue clutched in his hand.

"Are you fucking my wife?" he demanded, loud enough for anyone nearby to hear.

Daniel blinked. Then, slowly, he looked Mark up and down, unimpressed.

"Do I look like I'm fucking your wife?"

Mark's jaw clenched. "Don't play games with me," he hissed. "I saw her walk out of this room."

"So?" Daniel leaned against the doorframe, utterly unfazed. "Does that mean she was screwing me?"

Mark hesitated.

His plan to explode into a full-blown scandal hit an unexpected wall. Daniel didn't just answer him, he dismissed him. Calm. Unbothered and in control.

And Mark felt the shift. The invisible force pressed down on him clearly signaling that he wasn't the dominant one here. He hated it. And at the last moment, he backed down.

As he always did.

Something about Daniel, his presence, his unshaken demeanor made Mark feel small.
"We are not done" he said through the clenched teeth, turned away abruptly, marching back to his car. Before getting in, he threw one last grenade over his shoulder.
"Pack your shit, Ann. I want you out today."

She fixed him with a cold, unwavering stare. Then, her voice steady and firm, she said, "I'm leaving because I decided to. A long time ago."
He slammed the door shut and tore off down the road.

Before heading back to the neighborhood, Ann took a detour, driving past the motel along the road Mark had supposedly spotted her car from. It took her all of five seconds to confirm what she already suspected. There was no way he could have seen her from there.
So he was spying on me. The thought didn't enrage her as much as it should have. Instead, it

left her wondering, why? Mark had never struck her as the jealous type. Or maybe, after all these years, she didn't know him as well as she thought. But none of that mattered now. What mattered was the one line he'd thrown at her before leaving. "Pack your shit."

Fucker.

Ann's grip tightened on the wheel. My 'shit' is actually our two kids, you, jerk. She said it out loud, her voice filling the emptiness of the car.

She jabbed at the car's display, pulling up Jack's number. He picked up immediately.

"Ann, you're reading my mind. I was just about to call you."

"Oh yeah?" she said. "Well, I beat you to it. Mark kicked me out of the house."

Silence. Then Jack's voice, sharp with disbelief. "What? He had the guts to kick you out? Oh, fuck him. What a goddamn joke! Alright, I'm coming over."

"But it'll take you three hours, Jack."

"Not really," he said. "I'm in Toronto."

Ann exhaled. "Oh."

That changed things. She ended the call and headed straight for the school. It was time to pick up the kids.

***

Jack filled his father in on Ann's situation, and the McFadden family sprang into action. A few phone calls later, Scott found Meg, his cousin, lounging in the Florida sun, enjoying her newly purchased condo. Their conversation was brief. Meg, furious at Mark on Ann's behalf, didn't hesitate. Her townhouse, sitting empty until mid-May and thirty minutes away from Scott's grandkids' school, was Ann's for as long as she needed it. It was a relief, at least for a few weeks. For now, Ann had to focus on keeping the kids in school until Christmas break and then she could move back to Huntsville and start over.

Parked in the driveway of the house she had lived in for the past eight years, Ann took a moment before stepping out. The place looked different. Darker. Haunted. Heavy with secrets she no longer had to live with. Relief spread through her chest. In an hour, they'd be gone. Ann rested her hand on the door handle, willing herself to move.

Just say it.

She turned to the kids, mustering a smile. "Okay, you two. Time to get out, I have some news."
But even her smile couldn't smooth out the strain in her voice, the tension running just beneath it. The kids felt it instantly. Lily's eyes widened. Mark Junior frowned.

"We're moving today," Ann announced.

"Why?" Mark asked cautiously.

Ann took a breath. "Well, your dad and I had an argument, and he thinks we should stay somewhere else for a while. So here's the plan — until the Christmas break we'll stay at Aunt Meg's place, and then, we're moving to Grandpa Scott and Grandma Laura's."

Silence.

Lily was the first to speak, her voice low, almost a whisper. "Are you getting a divorce?"

Ann ran her palm over her jeans, a quiet gesture of distraction. "I don't know, honey. What I do know is that everyone needs a break."

Mark Junior shifted in his seat, then sat up straighter.

"Is Dad kicking us out? Just like that?" Mark Junior's voice was small, but the weight of his words hit Ann like a punch to the gut. Her throat tightened. She turned to them, forcing steadiness into her voice. "Don't say that, Mark. You two have nothing to do with this. It's between your dad and me." She swallowed hard. "Since I'm the one who takes care of you—school, sports, everything—you're coming with me."

A tear welled up, hot and heavy, slipping down her cheek before she could stop it. She blinked quickly, but it was too late. Two pairs of eyes locked onto hers, watching, waiting.

"Don't worry, Mom. We're with you. One hundred."

Ann let out a bitter smile. "One hundred what?"

Mark hesitated. "Uh… percent?"

"That's right," she said, fighting her tears back. "One hundred percent."

She reached for the door handle. "Let's go."

***

Her in-laws had managed to make her feel even worse than she already did. They weren't home. A deliberate move. No goodbyes, no well wishes, not even a forced, hollow acknowledgment. Just absence. A silent message that she and the kids meant nothing to them. Fine. She didn't care.

With the kids helping to pack their toys and school supplies, Ann had everything ready in about ninety minutes. Jack arrived soon after, and together, they loaded up two cars with suitcases and bags before pulling away from the house that was no longer hers. Spike claimed his spot for the ride between Mark Junior and Lily in the back seat.

Aunt Meg's townhouse was just twenty-five minutes away, and when Ann stepped inside, she found it in perfect shape. The house was clean, warm, and waiting. Her only task was to get the groceries. Leaving Jack and the kids to unpack, she headed for the store. On the way back, she made one last stop at the liquor store, grabbing a bottle of wine. She needed to celebrate.

***

The kids were asleep. Ann and Jack sat at the round glass kitchen table, the bottle of red uncorked between them. Spike settled comfortably under the table, nestled against Ann's feet. The gas fireplace bathed the room in warmth, making it feel almost like home. For the first time in days, Ann felt her body unwind. Jack, on the other hand, was fuming.

He had grilled her for details about Mark, about what happened, about how it all unfolded. So she told him everything. How she first started talking to Daniel on the trail. How he told her about the book he was writing, how she had unknowingly inspired his protagonist. How they met for coffee at The Coffee Master, where he handed her a fresh printout of his manuscript.

She told Jack how captivated she was by Daniel's book, how it was engaging, well-written, surprisingly compelling. They had started seeing each other more often on the trails, walking their dogs, discussing his story. And then, one day, Daniel didn't show up. Three days passed with no sign of him. Finally, she called him thanks to the fact that they had exchanged numbers. He sounded awful, told her he was sick, probably the flu. So she offered to drop off some medication and walk Betty. He didn't argue. And that was how she ended up at the motel. And how she found Mark parked outside.

Jack shook his head, his breath coming fast. 'He was definitely spying on you, Ann. She nodded, silent.

"I just don't get it. He's the one with things to hide, not you." Jack gave her a look, then stood and grabbed his laptop from his bag. He sat back down, flipping through folders. "Don't get mad, Ann, but Dad and I decided to keep an eye on Mark. Just to see what he was up to." He turned the screen toward her. "And I think I found something."

Ann looked at him, then at the screen. A photograph filled the display. It was Mark, walking into a downtown condominium. She frowned. "What is this?"

"This is where he's been going," Jack said. "Almost daily."

Ann tensed.

Jack clicked through more photos, more images of Mark entering the same building at almost the same time every day. "Out of eight workdays, he went there six times. Always between 2:03 and 2:07 PM."

Ann's pulse quickened. "Sounds like lunchtime."

Jack gave her a knowing look. "That's what I thought at first. But then I went inside, pretending to look for a place to eat. The concierge casually mentioned there were no restaurants in the building, just condos and a gym. That's when I figured Mark must have an apartment there. So after the third day, I started photographing everyone who entered before and after him, looking for a pattern."

He clicked one last time.

"Voilà," he said, leaning back. "Days four, five, and six—same woman. Always fifteen minutes before Mark."

Ann stared. Her breath caught. The image on the screen blurred for a moment before snapping back into sharp focus. Her mind tried to reject what she was seeing, but the evidence was right there. It was Daniela. Anthony's wife. The same woman Ann had met before, quiet and composed, always carrying an air of restraint, as if she held something back from the world.

"Oh my God." The words left her lips like a breathless whisper before the realization hit, sharp and sudden.

Niagara. Anthony. His disgusting proposition.

Of course. He knew. That bastard knew Mark was screwing his wife. "Fuck," she muttered.

Jack stretched out in his chair, watching her reaction. "I take it you know her."

Ann swallowed hard, nodding. "That's the wife of his friend and colleague."

Jack let out a short, humorless laugh. "Classic."

Suddenly, it all clicked. The little things. The ones she had noticed but brushed aside. The disappearing acts. His phone, always face down. The sudden weekend work trips. The endless late nights at the office. The way he casually turned down her lunch invitations whenever she happened to be downtown.

All of it had been in front of her the whole time. All these years Mark had been cheating on her with Daniela.

What a fucking prick.

Chapter 10

Dinner was quiet. The restaurant was half-empty, hushed conversations blending with the soft clink of silverware. Grace and George sat in a faintly lit corner, glasses of red wine in hand, untouched tiramisu resting before them.

Grace knew George wouldn't address the situation right away. He never did. He'd let the evening drag on, pretend to savor the wine, let her sit in silence, waiting. And then, just as she expected, he spoke.

"I take it the plan is for him to get a divorce and rid himself of that ungrateful bitch?"

Grace nodded. "Yes."

George swirled his wine, watching the deep red liquid catch the light. "Do you see a problem with that?"

Grace's voice was soft, almost pleasant. "There might be a problem. Her name's Daniela."

His face darkened, but he said nothing. Just shook his head. A long, heavy pause stretched between them before he finally spoke.

"Talk to him," he said, spooning into his tiramisu. "Tell him to stop." He glanced up at her. "And it's not a request, Grace."

She took a slow sip of her wine, then nodded. "Thank you for the decision. It makes things a lot easier for me."

George's lips curled into a dark, vicious smile. "Yeah. I will always make the decisions, Grace. Especially for you."

She smiled back. "Do you have another one for me tonight?"

"You bet," he said smoothly. "You're going straight to the basement when we're done here."

Grace's grip on the stem of her wine glass tightened. Just for a second. Not enough for anyone else to notice. Not even George. But she felt it. Grace lowered her gaze, took another sip of wine — rich, bold, intoxicating. She let the taste linger, savoring the anticipation.

Later that night, when Mark pulled into the driveway, Grace was waiting for him in the kitchen. She was calm, composed, and utterly satisfied, the lingering traces of George's discipline still imprinted on her body and mind. She leaned against the kitchen island, scrolling through her iPad. The door clicked shut. Mark stepped inside.

"Hey, Mom."

She looked up. He was pale, irritated, anxious.

"Is she gone?"

"She is. Took the kids too."

"That's expected," he muttered. "I'll deal with that later. Judges hate it when kids get yanked away from their mothers. I have to play it cool."

Grace moved to the coffee machine. "Want a cup?"

Coffee this late meant only one thing—a long conversation. Mark got the message. He climbed onto the highchair at the counter.

"Sure."

The rich aroma filled the kitchen, momentarily tricking him into feeling like it was just another morning. But it wasn't.

Grace set a cup in front of him and stood across the counter, cradling her own.

"Listen to me, son," she said, her tone even. "Like I told you before, you need to clean your backyard. No more Daniela. You need to lay low. We don't know what that cunning McFadden family has in mind. And I can feel it. They'll dig into you." She paused, giving him a measured look. "Especially her father."

Mark listened. It made sense. It all made sense. What didn't make sense, what threw him off, was how she knew about Daniela in the first place. But that wasn't the worst part. The worst part was that he had to stop seeing his slave. The one thing that gave him release. That let him be who he really was. Could he survive without it? Doubtful.

But his mother's voice was a warning, and the fear of his dirty secrets spilling into a divorce battle was stronger than desire. He snorted softly, barely concealing his frustration. "I'll take care of it, Mom."

"Good."

Grace turned to leave, then paused at the doorway. Without looking back, she said, "I had to take your car once, mine wasn't available. Needed tissues, so I checked the glove compartment. . Found a box. Saw that choker." A beat of silence.

"Then I saw it on her." Her voice remained casual, almost lazy.

"Two plus two makes four, Mark." She closed the door behind her.

Mark sat there for a long time. Thinking. His fingers twitched against the cup. That's how she knew. His mother played the long game here. She wouldn't have confronted him if she wasn't absolutely certain.

Then he thought about Ann. About the eight years she had given him. About how easy it was for her to leave. Because she never truly belonged in his world. He thought about the two incredible kids she had brought into his life. And about the one thing she never could give him. The one thing he needed. Ann wasn't a Master. But she sure as hell wasn't made to kneel either. And he had known that from the beginning. He had thought, foolishly, that he could live a normal life. That he could bury his true nature, be a good husband, play the part. But he had been wrong. Maybe it was in the genes. Not in the village genes, though. That thought had crossed him mind, too.

***

Ann drove back from the school, her hands steady on the wheel, but her mind anything but calm. The first morning at Aunt Meg's place had gone surprisingly smoothly. The kids were cooperative, stoic, even. No whining, no hassle. But Ann barely registered any of it. Her thoughts were consumed by last night's discovery.

Coincidences didn't exist. She knew that.

Daniela and Mark, arriving at the same condominium building, five minutes from his office, at the same time of day, six times in eight working days? There was no innocent explanation. Could it be rationalized? Maybe, if one believed in joint book editing sessions over lunch, a game of chess, or some entirely platonic reason for secretive midday meetings. But who would?

A man and a woman. Sinful as they are.

In ninety-five cases out of a hundred, they were sleeping together. The other five? Explained away by some kind of mental anomaly.

Ann clenched the steering wheel, forcing her focus back to the road. The clock read 9:05 AM. A thought struck her. She turned at the next plaza, pulling into a mobile phone shop. Fifteen minutes later, she walked out with a brand-new phone, a fresh SIM card, and a number no one wouldn't recognize.

By the time she got back to the townhouse, her plan was clear. Ann sat at the kitchen table, powered up the phone, and began typing. She crafted a message, disguising her true intent behind careful wording.

"Mr. Miller, I might have to take your suggestions seriously from our latest meeting at Two Sisters Vineyards, where you mentioned my lawyer did a lousy job. I totally agree. Please call me to discuss the arrangement. I'd prefer privacy as well."

Ann read it over one last time. Just cryptic enough. Just pointed enough. She pulled up Anthony's number from her old contacts, the one Mark had shared with her years ago, typed it in and hit Send. And just like that, the first domino fell.

**

The message hit Anthony like a detonated bomb. He knew instantly who sent it. But it was the meaning between the lines that truly electrified him.

Ann. Mark's wife.

The idea sent a jolt of exhilaration through him. He'd get to fuck Ann. That smug, self-righteous bastard's wife. He had always despised Mark — the snob, the prick, the weak man hiding behind pedigree, wealth, and an overplayed macho act that never quite fit. Their so-called friendship was built on convenience, but Anthony had seen glimpses of something darker in Mark over the years, something off. He just never managed to put his finger on it. But none of that mattered now.

Ann had sent him the message. From a new number. That meant preparation. Secrecy. A calculated step toward an affair. And if there was one thing Anthony excelled at, it was affairs. He had them down to a science, sometimes even running multiple at once, just like he would now. The Polish girl, his insatiable little addiction. And Ann would be the ultimate conquest. The final move in a game he'd been playing all along. The morning had just turned into the best day of his life.

The professional liar that Anthony always had been came with its perks. One of them being a collection of phones and numbers, each assigned to different women. The important ones got their own dedicated line, their own separate device. Like Melanie. Like Ann would.

It took him less than ten minutes to set everything up. He wasn't stupid enough to call from the office, where conversations could be monitored or, worse, recorded. The firm he worked for had airtight security policies, and he wasn't about to get sloppy. So he took the elevator to the fourth floor, where the snack bar and restaurant were, and tucked himself into a secluded booth.

He dialed the number Ann had used to message him.

She answered immediately.

"Hey there," he said, careful to keep his voice smooth, controlled, not betraying the rush of excitement surging through him.

"Hi." Ann's voice was unreadable.

"I'd really love to see you naked, ASAP" he said with his best seductive tone.

Ann didn't waste a second. "Drop the bullshit, Anthony. Did you actually think I was going to sleep with you? No fucking way. I need something else. Something important for both of us."

Anthony's heart plummeted. Fucking bitch. Played him again. The high, the anticipation vanished in an instant, evaporating like a trail of cigarette smoke, lingering just long enough to tease before disappearing completely. He swallowed his pride. "What is it? It better be good."

A pause. Then Ann said, voice eerily calm, "Actually, it's bad, Anthony. I just want to know something."

Anthony leaned back, his grip tightening around the phone.

"Back at Two Sisters," Ann continued, her tone razor-sharp, "when you had the guts to suggest I sleep with you, was that payback? For him fucking Daniela?"

The question hit like a slap.

"What?" Anthony barked, genuine shock slicing through his voice. "What the fuck are you blabbing about?"

Silence. A long, heavy silence. He could hear her breathing. She could hear his. Then, finally, she spoke.

"Right. I see how it is." Her voice was clipped, decisive. "Sherway Gardens. Thirty minutes."

The line went dead.

***

Their meeting lasted less than fifteen minutes. Ann placed her phone on the table, screen angled toward him and swiped through the photos one by one. Her voice was calm, deliberate, as she laid out the dates. Anthony barely moved. His eyes stayed locked on the screen, his fingers laced together, knuckles white.

"Why did you take these?" he finally asked.

Ann shrugged. "Kind of felt something," she said simply. "You know…"

He gave a slow, stiff nod, but his focus never left the images.

Daniela. His wife. The woman he had always considered quiet, refined, composed, mouldable like clay. And here she was, slipping into the same building as Mark, again and again. What a bitch.

His own affairs? Those were different. He was a man. He was wired for it. Hell, Daniela practically pushed him into other women's beds with how dull she was in his. But her? Anthony felt something cold and ugly settle in his chest.

When Ann left, he didn't move. He just sat there, the betrayal twisting into something darker.

Since he never truly loved Daniela, he saw an opportunity here, one too perfect to ignore. Take down that snobbish prick. Play the card of the devastated husband, deceived by both his wife and his so-called friend. What a script.

Mark would fall first—his reputation, his career, his polished image, all crumbling under the weight of a scandal too juicy to contain. And when the dust settled, Anthony would be there to pick up the pieces. He'd take Mark's place in the firm. He'd take his clients. He'd take everything. Maybe even Ann at the end of the day. He was sure he'd fuck her eventually.

He wanted revenge. A quiet, devastating one. But first, he needed proof. Bulletproof.

Chapter 11

Mark moved in restless circles, the dim glow from a single lamp in the far corner stretching his shadow across the scuffed wooden floor like a specter stalking his every step. The air was thick, humming with secrecy. And rightly so.

Kneeling before him, his pet remained still with her head bowed. She was trained well. Knew better than to move. Knew better than to speak.

Mark was on edge. What he had to say tonight would change everything. He debated the timing. Do it before or after the procedure? After a brief internal battle, he made his decision.

He stopped in front of her, close enough that her breath ghosted against his shoes.

Pause. Let her feel it. Let her anticipate.

"Listen carefully, pet." His voice was measured, smooth. "Something important has come up, and I need to stop seeing you for a while."

She tensed. A flicker, barely visible. But he saw it. Her breathing remained controlled, steady. Waiting. She wouldn't speak—not without permission. Instead, he watched her body for the only answers she was allowed to give. A tremor in her legs. The smallest dip of her head.

"I'm not letting you go," he continued.

"You belong to me. That won't change."
She barely moved, but he saw the way her breath caught, the way her fingers curled slightly against the cold floor.

"You'll have a secure phone," he said, flicking a card onto the floor. "A motel room. Paid for six months." Another card. "This unlocks the door." Her silence was predictable. She was waiting for his permission to react.

"When this is over, you'll leave Anthony. For good."

This time, she did react. A flicker of hesitation.

"You'll live in my house. Permanently." His voice was calm, controlled. "You're mine."

She inhaled sharply. Her body wavered between anticipation and submission.

He loved this moment where control became absolute.

"Are you pleased?" he asked.

A whisper. "Yes, Sir."

His eyes flicked to the table. The instrument of discipline. Waiting. He picked it up.

"Let's start."

She obeyed immediately. She always did.

And that's what he loved most about her.

***

Morning brought relief. The fever had broken, leaving only a dry cough and a strange weight in his limbs. But Daniel felt alive again. He glanced at the clock, yeah, he'd slept in, but his body had needed it. Still, there was time. Time to make it to the trail where Ann would be walking Spike.

He grabbed his keys, whistled for Betty. The motel door creaked as he stepped out, the late morning air still cold. Betty stretched at his feet, yawning before wagging her tail, eager to move.

The trail looked unchanged. Gold, brown, and orange still clung to the branches, though more leaves had fallen overnight, their damp scent rising up from the earth. Somewhere in the distance, a bird called out — a single sharp note in the quiet.

Ann was nowhere to be seen. Strange. He considered calling her, then dismissed the thought. After what happened at the motel, after her husband's scene, he didn't want to add any pressure. Instead, his mind drifted to their last meeting at the coffee shop. They had a few of them. They'd lost track of time, caught up in the book, in the conversation, in each other. When she finally glanced at her watch, realization hit.

"Oh my God, I have to run," she had said, pushing back from the table. But just before standing, her hand instinctively brushed his.

He hadn't moved. Hadn't spoken. Just met her gaze. For a split second, something hovered between them. A hesitation. A possibility. But then she withdrew, a flicker of embarrassment crossing her face. And that's when he did it. He reached forward, covered her hand with his.

"Not even five more minutes?" he asked, voice quiet.

She smiled. "I can do five."

He let go. So did she.

It had been a moment, small and fleeting, but it had shifted something. A crack in the walls they both had built. A step toward something neither of them had named yet, but both had undeniably felt.

Daniel's thoughts drifted back to the book. He was stuck on the fall. The woman had jumped or so it seemed. The mystery was there, but it felt too simple, too ordinary. It lacked something, and he couldn't quite grasp what. He had toyed with different ideas, but nothing stuck.

Then, he saw it.

A perfect golden leaf, clinging stubbornly to its branch, barely holding on as the wind threatened to rip it away. A day or two, and it would fall. Daniel watched, struck by its shape, its color, how impossibly golden it was. And then, the memory came. Not a real memory. Just a thought. A whisper of an idea.

The woman who fell... she must have been wearing something. Something important.

A necklace. Gold, delicate but striking. A maple leaf with a diamond at its center? His pulse quickened. A necklace? Yes. Beautiful maple leaf necklace! And huge diamond.

And when she fell the necklace was gone. Not lost. Not broken. Just... missing. Yes. Yes. He could see it now. Daniel tensed, a rush of adrenaline hitting him. That was the missing piece.

A strange thought wormed its way into his mind, unwelcome and unsettling. What if I'm not writing the story? What if I'm remembering it? A chill passed through him. He rubbed his palms together, a habit he had when he was uneasy.

Disappointed that Ann hadn't shown up but energized by his breakthrough with the necklace, Daniel drove back to the motel. As soon as he stepped inside, he opened his laptop, his fingers hovering over the keyboard for only a second before he started typing. The idea pulsed through him, electric. His mind raced, the words pouring out faster than he could catch them.

***

Ann finally called.

Daniel's pulse kicked up the moment he heard her voice.

"Sorry about the mess at the motel," she said. "Turns out it was enough to get me kicked out of the house. That's why I haven't been on the trails."

"Oh, wow." Daniel was stunned. "You're serious? He actually kicked you out?"

"Yes." Her voice was quiet but steady. "I'm staying at my aunt's place with the kids."

She paused, then, almost casually, added, "By the way, want to come over for tea? And maybe bring the rest of the book if you have anything new? I'll text you the address."

Daniel chuckled. "As a matter of fact, I do. Let me print everything out."

An hour later, they sat in the living room, sipping tea and unpacking the chaos of Ann's new reality.

"That's eerily similar," Daniel mused. "And kind of terrifying." He raked a hand through his hair. His old reflexive habit.

"First, I get kicked out of my house because of this manuscript. Then you get kicked out for bringing me cold meds. I mean—" he shot her a half-smile, "—is this book cursed? Some kind of dark magic at play?"

Ann shook her head, amused. "You have quite the imagination, Daniel. I think it's just life. Life always finds a way. This would've happened anyway, maybe not now, but eventually."

Daniel nodded and took a sip of tea. Then, flicking his gaze toward the manuscript on the coffee table, he joked, "Still, be careful reading that. Who knows what else it might set in motion?"

Ann laughed. "I'll keep that in mind."

The conversation drifted from the book to his past, and Daniel found himself telling Ann the story of his life.

He told her about his first marriage, the one that wasn't really a choice, but an outcome. A consequence of a summer romance between high school and university, a time when he and his high school sweetheart knew little about life, even less about sex, and ended up expecting a child before they had even figured out who they were.

Their parents got involved, and the only socially acceptable path was marriage. A baby on the way meant responsibility, and before Daniel could process what was happening, he was a husband, soon to be a father, and working himself to the bone just to keep them afloat.

Night shifts at a bakery. Early mornings cleaning equipment at a sports complex. Studying during the day. Their parents helped, but it was never enough. They grew up in survival mode, pushing forward without much time to think about the relationship itself. Romance and passion were shoved to the background. Years passed like that. Then, everything changed.

Daniel met a group of guys working in online business. He started helping them, learning the ropes, and before long, he saw an opportunity. He borrowed serious money from his uncle, from the bank, from every other possible source and went all in on his own project.

And somehow, it worked.

The first real money gave him freedom. His son's university was covered. Life should have gotten easier. But by then, his wife who, Daniel admitted, had probably wanted to add a small "ex" to her title for years, was already gone in her heart. She had found love. And she wanted out. She waited patiently for their son, Jakub, to turn 18. Then, she filed for divorce. Daniel had understood.

They parted amicably, no fights, no ugly battles. The same year she left, his business took off in a way he had never imagined. The kind of success that felt like a reward for years of hard work.

"That's such a story," Ann said, shaking her head. "You've been through a lot, Daniel. I guess your education saved you. Was it computer science?"

Daniel laughed. "That's the funny part, Ann. Imagine, I had nothing to do with any of this. My major was chemistry."

Ann blinked, genuinely surprised. "No way! You liked chemistry?"

"Loved it," he nodded.

She smiled but didn't push. Instead, she switched gears.

"And your second wife?"

Daniel's expression darkened.

"That's the classic case of me being an idiot," he admitted. "Falling for a much younger woman who played her cards right. Used me, used what I built, and secured her way into Canada."

Ann leaned in slightly. "So she knew exactly what she was doing," she murmured.

"Oh, she did," Daniel said. "Since we moved, I sold my property in Warsaw. We bought things here. And just like that, everything I had earned before she ever entered my life became shared assets in Canada. She found a way to push me out, and I'd bet my last dollar she's already thinking about her next target."

Ann nodded slowly.

"Life lessons," she said softly. "Why do we always have to learn the hard way?

They talked for a while longer before Daniel finally left, already hoping to see her again soon. Even before they'd spoken, Ann had somehow carved out a space in his mind. Now, she had cemented a place in his heart. And that space was growing. He was drawn to her, undeniably.

She was sharp, grounded, concrete. A steady force. A woman who wouldn't bend, wouldn't lie, wouldn't run. Unlike the ones before her. Unlike the ones who took everything and gave nothing back. Unlike the ones who saw trouble and chose the exit.

Anthony had a plan. A careful, calculated, and airtight plan. He would gather proof that Mark was involved with Daniela, build his case, and, when the time was right, take him down. But for now, he had to stay cool, stay patient.

The day dragged on. Anthony kept a close eye on Mark, waiting for him to slip, to make a move. But the bastard worked straight through, not even taking his usual lunch break, the one he always claimed to spend with his father's old friend downtown. Some lonely retired lawyer, supposedly. Mark had framed it as a kind gesture, a duty even, listening to the old man's stories over a meal. But that turned out to be total bullshit according to Ann's photos. Anthony never checked, he was too busy screwing around. But now, he would.

At the end of the day, Mark stepped into the elevator heading down to the parking garage. Anthony slipped in just before the doors closed. "Hey, buddy," he said casually. "What's the plan? Up for a couple of beers?"
Mark smiled. "Nah, thanks. Promised Mom I'd be home for dinner. Some kind of anniversary tonight." He laughed. "First kiss, first fuck, first

meeting or whatever it is, she made a big deal out of it."

Anthony chuckled along, masking his suspicion. "Next time, then."

They shook hands in the garage and went their separate ways.

Fifteen minutes later, Anthony was home. Mark's drive home should take him forty. Daniela wasn't home yet, he knew that much. He called her. She picked up on the third ring.

"What's up, baby?" she purred.

"Feel like dinner out tonight?"

"Mmmm," she murmured. "I'm meeting Rebecca in five. You should've given me a little notice."

Right. Anthony hung up.

Thirty minutes later, he dialed Mark's cell. Straight to voicemail. Interesting.

He tried Daniela again. Voicemail. Exactly.

One last attempt. He dialed Mark's home number.

Grace picked up. "Hello, Grace, this is Anthony."

"Oh, hi, darling! How are you?" Her voice was thick with sugar.

"I'm fine, Grace, you?"

"Not too bad. What can I do for you?"

"Ah, well, I was trying to reach Mark but his cell's off. He told me he was heading home for your anniversary dinner or something, so I figured I'd call the house."

A pause. Just for a second. But enough.

"Oh, that!" Grace recovered quickly, but Anthony had caught the hesitation. "We do have a little something to celebrate, but I may have exaggerated how important it is. We don't get to see him for dinners often, so I thought I'd guilt him into one." She let out a light, airy laugh.

Anthony played along. "Got it. Just let him know I called. I need one quick thing from him."

"Of course, darling."

She hung up.

Anthony sat back, rubbing his chin.

Mark had lied. Flat out. There was no anniversary dinner. His phone was off. Daniela's phone was off. They were sloppy. So obvious now that he was looking. Before, he had been too preoccupied covering his own tracks to notice theirs. Even now, in the middle of his so-called investigation, he had his own detour to take. Melanie. He needed to fuck her. And the big irony? She lived just a few houses down from Mark. Right across the damn street.

"Okay, Anthony, concentrate." He told himself. No mistakes. No risk. He wouldn't use his own car. Total secrecy. Anthony grabbed his phone and fired off a text: Pick me up at the GO station. Then he headed out the door.

***

Grace set the phone down and sank into the armchair.

"Fuck," she muttered under her breath.

Her fingers gripped the armrests as a slow, creeping chill spread through her body. A thin layer of cold sweat prickled at the back of her neck. The phone call had rattled her. Anthony was sniffing around. Something wasn't right. Could it have been an innocent, simple call? No way. Her gut told her otherwise.

How many times had Anthony called this house before? Zero. So why now? Because he was checking. Figuring out where Mark and Daniela were. Something must have happened.

Grace's mind raced. The only leverage she had, an ace up her sleeve, was Anthony's own indiscretion with the Polish girl, the neighbor. But that wouldn't be enough if he had real proof about Mark. And his call tonight left little doubt about that. He knew something. Maybe not everything, but enough.

She thought that Anthony had probably spent so much time juggling his own affairs, weaving alibis and keeping stories straight, that he never stopped to consider someone might be running their own game right under his nose. He had thought he was calling the shots, playing the game. Meanwhile, Mark, her son, had his wife on her knees. And no one had checked on anyone else because there was no need. Until now. So what the fuck had changed?

The floor creaked. Grace snapped her head up just as George stepped into the kitchen. Their eyes met. He read her face in an instant.
"Into my study," he said quietly, then turned and walked down the hall.

Chapter 12

The night air had turned sharp, dipping close to zero, and Ann felt the chill settle deep in her bones as she hurried Spike through his evening walk. She kept it brief—ten minutes at most. It wasn't just because of the cold. She hated leaving the kids alone in the house, even with them fast asleep. So she lingered just close enough to keep an eye on the front door, waiting for Spike to finish. He'd get his proper walk in the morning when they were at school.

Back inside, she shivered, flipped on the fireplace, and poured herself a glass of wine before settling onto the couch with Daniel's manuscript. He had printed the full version for her, unfinished but complete enough to pull her in. And it did.

There was something about it. The way it read, the way it felt. A strange magnetism she couldn't quite explain.

Even though it was fiction and his own imagined world, too many details rang disturbingly true. Small things. Nuances. And now, with what she had discovered about Mark, it was more than unsettling. The manuscript, which predicted Anna's husband had a mistress, had turned into a goddamn prophecy. She couldn't shake it. It made her uneasy. And yet, she needed to see it through.

And Daniel was quickly becoming one of the most fascinating people she had ever met. There was something about him, something she hadn't quite put her finger on. A man from Poland, from the other side of the world, only three years here, yet never a stranger to her. He didn't quite belong, not in the way people who had spent their whole lives in one place did. There was a certain restlessness in him, an awareness of being in transit rather than at home. And maybe that's why she never saw him as foreign. Because she felt it too. The quiet understanding that this place wasn't truly hers either.

The guy lived in a motel. That fact alone stirred something in Ann—sympathy, maybe. He had come to this country with his hard-earned money, built a life, only to have it dismantled piece by piece. His wife hadn't thrown him out overnight. No, it had been slower, more insidious. Conflicts engineered just right, tension dialed up degree by degree, until leaving felt like his only option. A careful kind of exile.

What a life, Ann thought.

And then, like a cold blade sliding in, the realization struck: wasn't her story the same?

She had married Mark, moved into his family's house, and from that moment on, the walls had been closing in. Not all at once, but little by little. A slow suffocation disguised as tradition, as duty. And when the time came, when they had finally squeezed her tight enough, Mark had done exactly what Melanie had done to Daniel.

The only difference was that Ann had somewhere to go. If she hadn't, she would have been in a motel too. Just like Daniel.

Ann shivered. Could Daniela be the real reason he kicked her out? Had he simply seized on her visit to Daniel's motel as the perfect excuse? And the way he had shown up, right on time, as if he had been waiting, watching.

So that was the plan. Find a reason. Push her out. Get the divorce. Settle with Daniela.

Ann dragged in a deep breath before turning her gaze back to the manuscript. Daniel's words had already predicted so much. Things he couldn't have possibly known. Maybe, somewhere in these pages, she'd find the answers she was missing.

Ann finished reading by 3 a.m., unable to put it down. The book was unfinished but undeniably racing toward its climax. Ann made a mental note to go over the most chilling parts with Daniel. Then, finally, she forced herself to sleep.

***

Grace arrived at the townhouse precisely at 9 a.m. She had called Ann the night before, asking if she could take the kids for the weekend. The request had surprised Ann, but she chose not to make things difficult.

"Sure," she had said.

The kids weren't exactly thrilled, but their father still had the right to see them. So, they packed their things and got ready for their first visit back to the house that no longer felt like home.

When Grace knocked, Ann opened the door swiftly.

"Morning, Ann," Grace said with a small, polite smile, just enough to be civil.

"Morning, Grace," Ann replied coolly. "Come on in."

Grace stepped inside, glancing around as Ann gestured toward the living room.

"Have a seat, I'll get them ready. Coffee?"

"I'm good, thanks," Grace answered, her tone clipped, restrained.

Ann simply nodded and went upstairs to make sure the kids had everything they needed. Less than ten minutes later, Grace and the children were gone, and Ann was left standing in the quiet, empty house. She got dressed, grabbed

Spike's leash, and took him for a walk. The morning was cool, the silence welcome.

When she returned, the burner phone, the one she used to communicate with Anthony, was ringing.

What now? she thought, fishing it from her purse.

"Hey, Ann," Anthony greeted her as she answered. "I just need a couple of minutes of your time. Can we meet?"

"Is it urgent?" she asked.

A slight hesitation. Then, his voice, uneven. "Quite. Yes."

Ann paused. She didn't feel like leaving the house. She didn't feel like inviting him in, either. But then again, what, ten, fifteen minutes?

"I'll text you the address," she said.

"Thanks," he replied, and the line went dead.

He arrived by Uber, stepping into the living room looking like hell, anxious, restless, his eyes darting, his face drawn and sunken, like he had aged a decade overnight. Ann handed him a cup of coffee and took one for herself, then sat across from him.

"Shoot," she said simply.

Anthony took a slow sip, like he was stalling, steadying himself.

"Does he know that you know?" he asked.

She shook her head. "No."

He let out a sigh of relief. "Okay. That's good."

A pause. He licked his dry, cracked lips and leaned forward slightly.

"I started digging, Ann. Checking things. Looking at patterns. They're definitely hooked. But it's worse than that."

Ann raised an eyebrow. "How much worse can it be?"

Anthony set his coffee down, pulled out his phone, and tapped the screen a few times before holding it out to her.

"I was fishing for clues, going through Daniela's things, checking her car when I could. And something told me to take a closer look at that choker she always wears when she leaves the house."

Ann glanced at the image on his screen. It was a close-up of the golden lock securing the choker at the back of Daniela's neck. It looked like the back side of the lock. And engraved into the metal was a single letter.

M.

Ann's pulse quickened. She looked back at Anthony, who was watching her reaction carefully.

"I dug around online," he continued, "and found out that certain types of chokers are used as symbols in… let's call them specialized relationships. The engraving here?" He nodded at the screen. "That's a signature. The mark of ownership. Whoever wears it is claiming possession by someone."

Ann's breath caught. It wasn't a smoking gun, not yet, but something deep in her gut twisted in recognition. She remembered Mark's clumsy but persistent attempts to control her, to mold her into something she wasn't. It all started to make sense.

She looked back at Anthony. "What's your agenda?" He met her gaze head-on. "Depends on where you stand, Ann. That's why I came here. I want to take him down. Ruin him. Strip him of his business, throw him out of the firm. I need to know—are you with me?"

Her thoughts spun.

Mark was the father of her children. Whatever he had done, his downfall would impact them too. But at the same time, stopping Anthony wasn't an option. He was going to do this, with or without her. Ann took a slow sip of coffee and set the cup down.

"Do what you have to do, Anthony," she said finally. "But don't count on my help."

He nodded, as if he'd expected that answer.

"Fair enough," he said, rising to his feet. "I wasn't expecting your help. I just need to know you won't get in my way."

With that, he was gone. The door clicked shut behind him, leaving Ann alone with the gravity of what she had just learned.

The Day of The Fall

The sky fell on Monday morning.

For Ann, it started with a terrifying headline flashing across her TV screen the moment she returned from walking the dog. A woman had fallen from an office building. Horrible. But what sent ice racing through her veins was the location. It was the same building that housed Mark's law firm.

Her pulse hammered as she grabbed her phone, searching for more details. Nothing. The news was repeating the same vague information—no names, no confirmations. She refused to call Mark, as she had no intention of speaking to him. Instead, she dialed Anthony. He worked in the same building, so he would know something.

No answer.

All day, a restless unease clung to Ann, shadowing her every move. It was there when she picked up the kids, when she drove them to sports practice, when she cooked dinner, and when she helped with homework. Something gnawed at the edges of her mind, refusing to let go.

And then, late at night, curled up on the couch with a glass of wine, it hit her like a hammer.

The Fall.

The manuscript. Oh, fuck, fuck, fuck.

A cold sweat broke across her skin. Her breath caught. Her hands trembled as she set the wine glass down. What if? What if it was Daniela?

The thought sent a full-blown panic spiraling through her chest. She told herself she was being irrational, that she was imagining things. But her body refused to believe it. Her eyes were already darting around the room, searching.

The manuscript. Where the hell was the manuscript?

She swore she had left it on top of the magazine pile in the wooden holder beside the couch. Or had she set it down in the kitchen? She rushed to check. Nothing.

Bedroom? She didn't remember bringing it upstairs, but she ran to look anyway. Empty.

Could the kids have taken it? She crept into their room, using her phone's flashlight to scan the floor, the nightstands, their shelves. Nothing.

The panic was clawing at her throat now. She ran back downstairs, her breath coming short and fast.

The manuscript was gone.

Her fingers fumbled for her phone. She dialed Daniel. Straight to voicemail.

Ann stood frozen in the dark living room, the world tilting beneath her feet. Something was very, very wrong.

She woke the next morning with a pounding headache and a gnawing sense of unease.

As soon as she dropped the kids at school, she dialed Anthony again. No answer. A bad sign.

Her phone buzzed just as she was about to try again. Daniel.

"Hey, Ann. Sorry I missed your call last night," he said. "I was working late, didn't notice my battery died."

"No problem," she said, though her voice was tight. "I... I just wanted to ask. Did you see the news? About the Fall?"

There was the briefest pause.

"What fall?"

"The woman from the office building. The skyscraper," she said.

"No," he replied, too calm. Too calm.

"Why?" he asked. "What happened, Ann?"

A lump formed in her throat. "It made me uneasy, Daniel. Because... because... look, that building is where my husband works." She hesitated, then pushed out the words. "And your manuscript... Daniel, it's exactly the same."

A beat of silence. Then a soft, disbelieving laugh. "Oh, come on, Ann. It's fiction. Pure imagination. You can't seriously think—"

"Daniel." Her voice was firm. "Do you really believe in coincidences like this?"

He hesitated, thinking. Then, finally. 'Me? No."

Silence stretched between them, thick and heavy. Then, almost under his breath, he muttered, "What the fuck is wrong with this manuscript?" His tone wavered between uncertainty and forced amusement, like he wasn't sure whether to be spooked or brush it off as a joke.

Ann wasn't joking.

"We'll find out soon enough," she said.

That day, Ann tried reaching Anthony seven more times. Each call went unanswered. Finally, with growing reluctance, she dialed Mark. No answer.

By the end of the day, frustration gnawing at her, she resorted to the last person she wanted to call, Grace.

"Hello, Ann." Grace's voice was cool, detached.

"Evening, Grace. Sorry to bother you. I saw the news about the woman who jumped from Mark's office building, and I just... I wanted to make sure everything was all right. I mean..."

Grace cut her off. "Yes, I heard. But Mark flew to Boston Sunday afternoon for business. He's still there. Comes back tomorrow. He wouldn't know anything about it."

Ann felt foolish. Of course, calling Grace had been a mistake. "Oh, I see. Well, sorry to bother you. Have a good night—"

But Grace wasn't done.

"Hold on a second." Her voice sharpened. "Why are you so fixated on this woman? Did you have something to do with it?"

Ann froze. "What?"

"You heard me," Grace said smoothly. "You sound unusually engaged in this incident."

Ann's pulse kicked up. "No! I just saw the news, realized it was Mark's office, and—"

"And what, Ann?" Grace pressed. "You do seem awfully invested."

"Good night, Grace." Ann hung up.

Her hands trembled as she set the phone down. What a bitch.

She clenched her jaw, then cursed herself. First for making the call, then for letting her mind spiral. The manuscript, the news, the eerie coincidences... it was twisting reality, pulling her into something irrational. She needed to stop.

She swallowed two Tylenol, climbed into bed, and forced herself to sleep.

Chapter 13

It was almost noon, and Ann was cleaning the kids' room when she heard a car pull into the driveway. Curious, she glanced out the window and froze. A woman stepped out, opened the back door, and out jumped Betty, Daniel's lab.

Ann's stomach clenched. Something was wrong. The woman clipped the leash, keeping Betty close, and walked up to the front door, pressing the bell.

Ann barely felt her feet as she hurried down the stairs, her pulse hammering. She yanked the door open.

"Ann McFadden?"

"Yes," Ann's heart skipped a beat.

"I'm Detective Julia Ricci, Homicide Unit, Specialized Criminal Investigations, Toronto Police. May I come in?"

Ann couldn't speak. She simply stepped aside, letting Julia and Betty enter.

"I see you recognize the dog," Julia said.

Ann nodded. "She's Daniel's."

"That's right." Julia studied her.

Ann swallowed. "Is he... dead?"

Julia's expression didn't shift. "Why would you assume that?"

Ann hesitated. "You brought his dog. That means he can't take care of her."

"No," Julia agreed. "He can't. He's in custody."

Ann's breath caught. "What? What did he do?"

"I can't discuss that," Julia said smoothly. "But I do have a few questions. Would you mind?"

Ann shook her head. "No, of course not."

She motioned for Julia to take a seat while Betty, overjoyed to see someone familiar, pressed herself against Ann's legs. Spike, who had been dozing under the table, ambled out, wagging his tail as he and Betty greeted each other.

Julia sat on the couch, her posture sharp, businesslike. "Tell me about Daniel. What do you know about him?"

Ann hesitated, deciding where to start. "We used to live on the same street. That's how we met, walking our dogs on the trail. He moved out a few weeks ago to a motel. I moved here to my aunt's place. He's from Poland, came to Canada three years ago with his wife... who later kicked him out. That's what he told me."

Julia's gaze sharpened. "Do you know why? Were there tensions? Fights?"

"I don't know the details," Ann admitted. "But I do know they argued a lot. And then... she found his manuscript."

Julia raised a brow. "Manuscript?"

"He was writing a book. A love story turned thriller. When she found it, she claimed... well, she said it was proof he was in love with me."

Julia didn't react, just took a slow sip of her coffee. "In love with you? Why would she think that?"

Ann's cheeks burned. "He didn't know me then. Not really. He just... imagined things. He'd see me walking my dog, and somehow, I became the heroine of his story. He described me in such detail that when his wife read it, she immediately knew."

"Are you two involved?" Julia's voice was level. "Sexually?"

Ann stiffened. She hesitated for a long slow second. Finally she said "No. Nothing like that. We're just... friends. He gave me the manuscript to read. That's all. I helped him with Betty once, brought him some medicine when he was sick."

Julia nodded, taking that in. "Can I see the manuscript?"

Ann bit her lip. "That's the thing. A few days ago, he gave it to me, and I read it... but now it's gone. Missing."

"Gone?" Julia's voice sharpened. "You mean lost? Or stolen?"

"I don't know," Ann admitted. "I just know I can't find it."

"That's… interesting," Julia murmured.

Ann hesitated. "That manuscript… it shook me."

"Why?"

Ann looked at her. "Because of the plot. The heroine's husband has a secret mistress. Then, one day, the mistress jumps from a building, the same building where the husband's office is." She swallowed hard. "And Monday morning, I saw the news."

Julia's eyes widened.

"A woman jumped," Ann whispered. "From my husband's office building. Just like in Daniel's book."

For the first time, Julia looked rattled. She stared at Ann, processing. Either this was a bizarre coincidence… Or she had just found the thread that would unravel everything.

Something in Julia's gut told her to hold off on more questions. She had already uncovered a crucial piece of the puzzle, the manuscript.

Daniel Nowak's laptop needed to be examined.

She'd take it to the judge. Or maybe she'd speak to Daniel first. She would decide soon enough.

Julia stood. "Please don't discuss this with anyone," she said, slipping a business card onto the coffee table. "I have a feeling I'll be seeing you again."

Ann only nodded.

Julia clipped the leash from her wrist and handed it over. "Betty's yours for now."

Before leaving, Julia paused at the door, her gaze fixed on Ann with quiet scrutiny. She was weighing the woman in front of her. Was Ann simply someone who had been unwittingly pulled into a web of chaos? Or was she holding something back, telling only half the truth? Then with a nod she closed the door.

Ann sank onto the couch. The world was disintegrating before her eyes. It felt like an avalanche, roaring down the mountain, unstoppable, devouring everything in its path.

Ann grabbed her phone and dialed Scott.

"Dad, I need your help."

Chapter 14

Julia stepped back inside, letting the silence of the crime that still hung in the house settle around her as she flipped through her notes. She moved slowly, her mind sifting through the details — Daniela Miller, the missing choker, the conversation with Ann McFadden.

And now, the manuscript.

It had surfaced like a ghost from the shadows, tying itself to the case in ways that didn't feel like mere coincidence. Ann had been visibly rattled, almost unnerved, by the book Daniel Nowak had been writing. She claimed the Fall, the exact kind of death that had rocked the city two days ago, was described in its pages.

But was it a connection, or just an eerie stroke of fiction colliding with reality?

Julia needed to talk to Daniel. She knew it would be a long conversation, but it could wait until later. For now, she moved through the house, taking in every detail, scanning for anything she might have missed.

Two empty bedrooms, nothing of interest. The master bedroom, where Melanie and Anthony had been murdered, had already been combed over, cataloged, and analyzed down to the last detail. Still, she took a final look, just in case.

Then she stepped into Daniel's study. A desk, a chair, an IKEA bookshelf filled with books, nothing unusual. Julia ran her fingers along the spines, scanning the titles. Next to the bookshelf, a small bedside table had been repurposed as a printer stand. She opened its drawers. Paper, stationery, the usual clutter.

And then she saw it.

A few loose pages, half-hidden beneath the bottom shelf as if they had slipped down when the drawer was full. Or maybe they hadn't just slipped. Maybe someone had shoved them there. Julia carefully removed the drawer and retrieved the pages. One glance was enough. She was holding Daniel Nowak's manuscript.

Julia sank into the chair and started reading. Page by page, her eyes scanned each sentence, missing nothing. She was methodical. Precise. She had neither the luxury nor the time to linger on every word, so she fished for important, key details, absorbing them with professional detachment, until she wasn't.

She stopped cold. The Fall. The scene on one page made her pulse stutter.

A woman. An office building. The plunge.

And then, finally, the choker.

A slow, crawling chill spread through her chest. The description: the shape, the design, the colors wasn't just similar. It was exact. It was Daniela Miller's. The same one she had been wearing when she walked into that office building. The same one that had vanished from her body after the fall.

Julia swallowed hard, her fingers tightening around the paper as if anchoring herself to reality.

"Holy fuck," she muttered under her breath.

She snapped the pages into her bag and shot to her feet. Moving quickly, she locked the front door, strode to her car, and slid behind the wheel.

Daniel Nowak's 24-hour hold was running out.

She needed to see the judge. Now.

***

Scott McFadden called his daughter early that morning.

"Ann, I don't have the news yet, but Alison is on it. I'm sure she'll find out."

Alison, Aunt Meg's daughter, was a high-ranking official in Ottawa, working for the Ministry of Foreign Affairs. Scott had called Meg, who then reached out to Alison, asking her to dig into who had died in the Fall. It was a long shot, but the only one the McFadden family had. Alison wasn't in law enforcement, not even close, but she had connections.

"Thanks, Dad," Ann sighed. "This whole thing makes me really nervous. I feel like I'm in the middle of a storm that's about to rip my life apart."

Scott's voice was calm, unwavering. 'Whatever happens, Ann, we're here for you. We stand by you, and we'll protect you and the kids. I really think the best thing now is for you to come back home to Huntsville. Forget school. Christmas is around the corner. There's no need to wait."

Ann pressed her lips together, thinking. "I agree. I should start packing. I'll be home by Friday."

"Good," Scott said. "I'll call you the minute I hear anything from Alison."

Ann slipped her phone into her purse and grabbed her car keys. She needed to run out for groceries. But the moment she opened the door, she froze.

Julia Ricci stood on her doorstep.

"Morning, Ann," Julia said, her tone casual but her eyes sharp. "Would you mind if I steal ten minutes of your time?"

Ann hesitated for a fraction of a second before stepping aside. "Sure."

She led Julia into the house, and they settled on the same sofa where they had spoken the night before.

"Something came up," Julia began, her voice measured. "I wanted to discuss it with you."

Ann nodded, waiting.

Julia leaned in slightly. "You mentioned the manuscript last night. Can you tell me more about it? In detail."

Ann blinked. "More? You mean... the plot?"

"Yes," Julia said. "Everything you remember."

Ann pressed her lips together, gathering her thoughts. "Well, it's about a woman named Anna. She's unhappily married, trying to figure out what went wrong, analyzing her husband, questioning herself. She finds signs and clues that her husband might be having an affair with someone. Then, out of nowhere, a woman dies.

She jumps off the roof of the office building where Anna's husband works, and the investigation begins. There's a witness, someone who was in the elevator with Anna just before she went up. The witness, another woman, tells the police she remembers a striking necklace. A maple leaf with a large diamond around Anna's neck. But when they find the body, the necklace is gone. That's where it ends. At least, that's as far as Daniel had written."

Julia didn't take her eyes off Ann's face, absorbing every word with an intensity that made Ann shift slightly in her seat. And then, Julia delivered the blow.
"What about the choker?"
Ann's expression changed in an instant. Julia caught it. There it is.
She didn't know what Ann knew, but she knew the word had hit a nerve. And that was enough.

"The choker?" Ann's voice barely held steady.
"Yes," Julia said, her gaze unrelenting. "Black and gold. A golden lock in the middle."
Ann's chest tightened, air suddenly hard to draw in. The room tilted. A cold wave of nausea rolled over her, threatening to pull her under. She lowered her head, pressing her palms against her

temples, trying to steady herself, trying to breathe.

"Oh my God," she whispered. "Oh my God."

When she finally lifted her eyes to Julia, they were brimming with tears. Her voice, barely more than a breath, trembled with the weight of realization.

"It was Daniela, wasn't it?"

They sat at the kitchen island, both gripping glasses of water. Ann had finally calmed down.

"When I heard it on the news and saw it was Mark's building," she began, her voice steadier now, "something in me just... knew. The mind games with that manuscript started playing tricks on me, and I was afraid, deep down, subconsciously, that it was Daniela. By then, I already suspected Mark was sleeping with her, especially after Anthony came by and showed me the photo of the engraving on the back of that choker's lock."

Julia remained silent, absorbing every word.

Ann shook her head, frustration tightening her voice. "As soon as I saw the news, I called Anthony, but he never answered. Never called back. And I figured... he was avoiding me. Either because he didn't want to share what he knew, or..." She hesitated, rubbing her temple. "Or something worse. He wanted to take Mark down. Seriously, take him down."

Julia studied Ann, weighing her next move carefully. She knew when to drop a bombshell, and this was the moment.

"This manuscript, and Daniel in general," Julia said, her tone calculated. "Do you believe he could be connected to all of this?"

Ann hesitated, searching for an answer she didn't have. "I—I don't know. I mean, the manuscript reads like it's predicting real events. How is that even possible?" Her brows knit together. "But at the same time, Daniel had nothing to do with me and Mark before this. I can't see how he'd be involved. I just—" she sighed, frustrated. "I don't know."

Julia nodded slowly. Then, with measured precision, she said, "And Anthony never answered your calls?"

Ann shook her head. "No. Not once."

"He wouldn't," Julia said. "Because he's dead."

A hollow gasp left Ann, as if the air had been punched from her lungs.

Julia didn't stop. "Along with Daniel's wife, Melanie. They were killed at Daniel's house. In bed. Together."

Ann's eyes widened in pure, raw shock. She didn't move, didn't even breathe for a second.

Her pulse roared in her ears. When she finally managed to swallow, her voice was barely a whisper.

"Do you... do you know who killed them?"

Julia leaned in slightly. "Think about it, Ann. A husband and his lover are murdered in bed. The husband's wife then jumps from a building. As if out of guilt, right?" She let that sit for a moment before continuing.

"But then," Julia said, her voice dropping slightly, "We have Daniel who wrote a manuscript describing that goddamn choker in perfect detail, almost as if he had it. And now you're telling me that in his manuscript, it wasn't a choker. It was a necklace. So that means there are two versions. Identical stories, except for that one key difference."

Julia locked eyes with Ann.

"So, you tell me, Ann" she said, her voice low, deliberate. "Who killed them?"

Ann could barely process the question, let alone answer it. Her mind reeled, spiraling through the chain of events, the connections, the impossibilities that no longer felt impossible.

She swallowed hard, her voice a breathless murmur.

"I... I have no idea."

Julia's phone shattered the silence. Ann flinched, a shiver running through her. Julia glanced at the screen. Gustavo, her assistant, was calling.

"I need to take this," she said, already pushing up from her chair. She stepped away, moving toward the living room windows.

She swiped the green button. "Go ahead."

Gustavo's voice came through, steady and businesslike. "Got some updates, boss. First, with the judge's permission, we had Nowak's laptop analyzed. The manuscript file is there, but there's a different version: the necklace. Maple Leaf with a diamond. No mention of a choker anywhere in the system. The IT team ran every kind of search. Nada."

Julia huffed. 'Uh-huh."

And then," Gustavo continued, "we got his immigration file. Mostly standard stuff, nothing interesting, except one detail that might be big." He paused. "He studied at Warsaw University. Faculty of Organic Chemistry."

Julia went still. Her mind processed the implications fast. "Right," she said, her voice measured. "That's… quite the development."

"Thought you'd think so," Gustavo said.

"Anything else?"

"That's it for now."

"Send me the immigration file. I want to go through it myself."

"Already on it, boss."

Julia ended the call, her expression unreadable as she turned back to the kitchen. Ann was still frozen in place, staring at the wall like the weight of everything had finally knocked her breath out.

Chapter 15

Mark was in Boston. The last-minute trip had been triggered by an urgent call from an old client, one of his best, a man who had once worked with Mark's father before seamlessly transitioning his business to Mark. Peter Wallen. Old money. Old ties.

Peter was in pharmaceuticals, operating at a level where contracts were massive. Both private and government sectors funneled billions through his network. Big money. Huge. The kind that didn't only buy luxury but influence.

Mark flew out Sunday afternoon and met Peter for dinner. Over steaks and a bottle of Bordeaux, Peter laid out the issue. Mark listened intently, but the more Peter spoke, the clearer it became that the man's in-house lawyers could have handled this. Easily. It wasn't an emergency. But Mark didn't say a word. Peter was too valuable, too connected. Too important for his future.

After dinner, Peter drove him back to the hotel and, before dropping him off, asked, One more? The hotel bar stocks a Macallan that'll spoil you for anything else. Mark didn't hesitate. "Absolutely."

They settled back into business talk over crystal glasses of scotch. One round turned into two. Then three. Mark leaned back in his chair, letting the warmth of the liquor settle in, when he noticed her.

A brunette. Striking. Unmistakably beautiful.

She sat alone in the corner, nursing a martini, her posture effortlessly poised, her gaze occasionally drifting over the rim of her glass. Mark stole a glance. Then another. He didn't imagine it. She had noticed him, too.

When Peter finally called it a night, Mark walked him to the front door, shook his hand, and bid him goodnight. But instead of heading upstairs to his room, he turned back toward the bar.

She was still there.

Mark approached, smooth and direct. "Would you like some company?"

She looked up, studied him for a moment, just long enough to make him wonder what she'd decide and then smiled and motioned to the empty chair across from her.

"Please," she said.

Mark waved to the bartender, signaling for another round of their drinks, then slid into the seat.

"I'm Mark," he said. "From Toronto."

"I'm Bella," she replied. "From Miami."

"Miami," he mused. "Sounds warm."

She laughed. "You're cute."

"Thanks," he said with an easy smirk. "You're lovely."

The bartender arrived with their drinks. They clinked glasses.

And just like that, the night had begun.

***

Mark woke late, his head pounding but his mood soaring. What a night. He felt like he'd just walked away from a high-stakes table with a million-dollar win.

Bella.

The stunning brunette with a body men would kill for had been more than just mind-blowing sex. She had sent all the right signals, hinted at her preferences, and played into his desires better than he could have scripted. Honestly, she was a goddamn gift.

Daniela suddenly became a distant memory. Boring, even.

And Ann... well, Ann didn't even belong in the same conversation. She could never match this.

Mark stretched, turning onto his side. Bella lay beside him, tangled in the sheets, her slow, steady breathing a sign of deep, satisfied sleep. He reached for his phone on the bedside table and swiped through the notifications.

A text from Bobby, his personal assistant:
"Quite a morning at the building, boss. Some girl jumped. Police, medics. Hell of a mess."

Mark frowned. Damn. Poor soul. He scrolled through the news, checking for more details, but nothing stood out yet. No name, no photo. Just another tragic fall.

He shifted to his emails, then his social media accounts. All clear. His meeting with Peter was set for 3 p.m. Plenty of time to shake off the hangover and be back in top form.

Mark turned his head, eyes trailing over Bella's bare shoulder. A slow grin spread across his face. Maybe round two before breakfast.

***

Mark could have wrapped up Peter's legal concerns in twenty four hours, max. It wasn't even a complicated issue, just another case of a pharmaceutical giant covering its ass. One of Peter's companies had developed a drug with questionable side effects, and he wanted to ensure his legal safety net was as tight as possible. Mark's job was simple: review what Peter's in-house lawyers had done and make sure they hadn't missed anything.

For someone of Mark's caliber, it was child's play. But Mark had no intention of rushing.

Bella.

She was still in Boston for another week, and that gave him the perfect excuse to stretch out his time here. He'd keep Peter occupied just enough to justify billing extra hours while indulging in his newfound entertainment. It was shaping up to be a damn good vacation.

Until everything exploded.

Two days later, the firm got a call from the Toronto police.

Anthony Miller, one of their top lawyers, had been murdered.

The firm scrambled for details, and it didn't take long to uncover the full catastrophe. The woman who had jumped from the office building? Daniela Miller. Anthony's wife.

Mark sat in his hotel room, glued to his phone, piecing it together through frantic calls and hushed conversations. Daniela had apparently discovered Anthony's affair with another woman. A woman who, by some twisted coincidence, had lived on the very same street as Mark. Sometime after that revelation, she had killed them both in bed. And the next morning, she had thrown herself off the building.

Mark leaned back against the headboard, running a hand over his face. What a fucking twist. At first, the sheer shock of it was enough to leave him stunned. But as the initial adrenaline wore off, his mind sharpened. He could already see the angles, the opportunities.

This wasn't bad at all.

No more Daniela. Just the way Mom had wanted.

No more divorce drama with the McFaddens digging for dirt.

Anthony's high-profile clients would most likely migrate to Mark.

And the cherry on top? He had already found something much better than Daniela.

Bella. Bellissimo.

But something didn't sit right with Mark.

Worse, he knew exactly what it was.

The circulating theory, the neat little package of murder-suicide, wrapped up with a bow, was utter bullshit. Because of Daniela.

He knew her. And no matter what anyone said, he knew one thing for certain. She wasn't a killer.

Not in a million fucking years.

She wasn't capable of something like that. Cold-blooded. Calculated. Methodical. That wasn't Daniela. It never had been.

So the dark, suffocating cloud that loomed over his newly found Boston freedom wasn't paranoia. It was certainty. It was fact. And no matter how hard he tried to ignore it, it followed him, gnawed at him, stole his sleep. Someone had killed them. Someone had orchestrated this whole goddamn thing.

And the only questions that mattered now, the ones that clawed at the edges of his mind every waking second were Who? And why?

Mark knew from his sources that Anthony's lover's husband was in custody. So, theoretically, it could have been him. A crime of passion. A man pushed too far.

But there was the timeline... And that was the part that gnawed at him. How plausible was it that these were two entirely unrelated events? Anthony and Melanie weren't victims of murder, they were executed for their sins. And then, mere hours later, Daniela plunged to her death. Coincidence? Coincidences sometimes happened. But Mark wasn't naive. This was no fucking coincidence.

Chapter 16

The first snow dusted the trail in white, softening the world around Ann as she walked both dogs, Betty and Spike. Surprisingly, they behaved. Especially Betty. She missed Daniel.

She missed him in the quiet, in the way Betty barely ate, in the way the dog curled up by the fireplace, restless, lifting her head at every car that pulled into the row of townhouses. Every time, she'd jump up, rush to the window, ears perked, tail hopeful only to return to her spot with a quiet sigh of disappointment.

Ann knew the feeling.

Ann's mind wouldn't stop. The burden of it all settled over her, dense and unrelenting, refusing to let go. She knew Mark was in trouble. That much was clear. She had told Julia everything. About the pictures Jack took, the choker, the engraving Anthony had discovered. She didn't hold anything back. She knew she'd be on the suspect list, too. Her husband had likely been sleeping with the dead woman, after all.

But she wasn't afraid. She knew she didn't do it.

She wasn't so sure about Mark.

And she wasn't so sure about Daniel, either.

Ann cursed that goddamn manuscript.

Why the hell did Daniel have to write that book?

Scott finally called with the news Ann already knew. She thanked him, then told him she wouldn't be coming on Friday because Detective Ricci had specifically asked her not to leave the area.

"Then we're coming to stay with you," Scott said, leaving no room for argument. Ann sighed but didn't fight it.

"See you soon," she said and clicked off.

She needed time to think. To sort through the chaos unraveling around her. She was uncertain of who to trust, what to believe, or even what to do. Not that she had any control over it.

The silence of the trail, the slow drift of tiny snowflakes, created an eerie sense of calm. A false serenity, but one she was desperate to hold onto. Right, Ann thought, almost speaking the word aloud. She needed to start somewhere.

Daniel.

Could he have killed them?

The thought sat uneasily in her mind. Nothing about him ever struck her as violent. He was kind, soft-spoken, even gentle. A man who spent his time writing a book, walking his dog, and quietly accepting the wreckage of his marriage. If anything, he had seemed resigned, choosing to leave his own home rather than fight Melanie for it. He could have stayed. He could have pushed her out. But he didn't. Even when Melanie humiliated him in public, he had stayed calm. Like he had already decided he was done. She knew he had lost at least half of everything he built, yet he wasn't bitter. He was searching for a way forward, trying to rebuild. Everything about Daniel screamed innocence. Except for the fucking manuscript.

Then there was Mark.

Could he have killed Daniela?

Ann hesitated, biting her lip. Deep down, she had always believed Mark was weak. She doubted he had it in him to kill. Then again, she had also doubted he would cheat on her. And he had. If he could prove he had truly been in Boston, just as Grace claimed, he would be off the suspect list.

Then came the million-dollar question.

Who did it? And why? Or maybe it was exactly what it seemed. Daniela had killed her husband and his lover. And then, drowning in guilt, she had jumped. The most logical theory. But then why didn't it feel right?

Ann walked back to the house, fed the dogs, and headed out to the grocery store. Her parents were arriving tonight.

***

The cell was sterile, the faint smell of antiseptic clinging to the air. More importantly, it was empty, except for Daniel. And for that, at least, he was grateful. No cellmate. Not yet. But even if he had one, it wouldn't have distracted him from the thoughts weighing him down.

And they weren't pleasant.

Sitting here, locked away, was the final, crushing blow to his life in Canada. A downfall, so sharp and brutal that he could hardly process it. A man like him, educated, decent, raised in a good Catholic family, was now sitting in a jail cell like a common criminal. It was unthinkable. He had never been ready to fall this low, this fast. But sometimes, he thought bitterly, our passions lead us to ruin. His own had dragged him straight to rock bottom.

He sat on the edge of the cot and covered his face with his hands. He replayed it all in his mind, the moment his world cracked open.

The call had come from Melanie's office. Someone looking for her, sounding casual, even friendly, asking if he had another way to reach her since she wasn't answering her phone. That was the first sign of trouble. They were separated, yes, living apart, but it wasn't like her to be completely unreachable. His gut had twisted. Something felt wrong. He told them he'd check.

His heart had been pounding by the time he reached the house. From the outside, everything looked normal. Then he saw the Nest camera by the door, covered with black tape.

A robbery? No. This was worse.

His fingers shook as he punched in the code. The lock whirred, the door swung open, and he stepped inside. "Melanie!" His voice rang through the house. Nothing. Silence. A silence so thick and unnatural it sent ice down his spine.

He searched the first floor. Empty.

Then he climbed the stairs.

At the bedroom door, he froze.

The scene before him was something out of a nightmare. Melanie, stark naked, lying on the bed. Beside her, a man, a stranger, his toned body half-covered by the sheets. Both of them still. Too still. Their faces peaceful, as if simply sleeping. But Daniel knew. He knew the moment the stale, cloying scent of death hit him.

His stomach twisted violently, and he doubled over, vomiting right there in the hallway. He didn't go closer. Didn't check for pulses. He already knew.

Stumbling back down the stairs on unsteady legs, he threw open the front door, gasping for air. His hands were shaking as he dialed 911.

And then, as the weight of what he had just seen crashed down on him, Daniel sat on the doorstep and cried.

He cried for Melanie. For himself. For everything that had led him here.

Before the police arrived, Daniel's mind was a storm of confusion. His first thought wasn't murder. It must have been an accident. An overdose. That's what the scene looked like. Two bodies, side by side, lifeless but undisturbed. It hadn't struck him as a crime, not at first.

The black tape over the Nest camera had to be Melanie's doing. It made sense. She had access to the security system just as he did, but she wouldn't have known how to revoke his permissions. The easiest solution would have been to cover the lens. That way, Daniel wouldn't be able to check the recordings and see who had been coming and going from the house. Who she had been sneaking in.

But when Detective Ricci arrived and declared it a double homicide, Daniel's world tilted.

Murder?

The word sent a bolt of panic through him. Who the hell would have done this? Who would have killed Melanie? Shock rendered him mute. He barely reacted when they cuffed him, barely registered the drive to the station. He hadn't fought it, hadn't objected. He knew how these things worked. He was innocent and in 24 hours, he'd be out.

But then, the unimaginable happened. The judge extended his detention. And just like that, Daniel Nowak was no longer a man answering questions. He was their prime suspect.

Now, in this cold, empty cell, he made himself a promise: If he got out of this, if he survived this, he would start over. He would climb back up. He would make different choices.

No more chasing shiny things. No more mistaking illusions for something real.

Because the life he had built with Melanie, the compromises he had made, the values he had traded for the sake of being with a beautiful woman who offered great sex and a glamorous life, had just spectacularly backfired.

And that, at least, he understood.

***

Julia Ricci gathered her team for a brainstorming session. Gustavo and Keelan, her two lead officers on the case, sat across from her, their notepads ready. She was preparing to interrogate Daniel Nowak, and she needed to be sharp. Every angle had to be covered, every inconsistency addressed. This was the moment to step back, reassess, and break the case wide open.

"Gustavo, let's run through everything," Julia said, leaning back in her chair. She preferred listening to a review rather than leading it herself—it helped her catch discrepancies, gaps, and doubts. She was a listener, and a damn good one.

Gustavo drummed his fingers on the table, a thick case file spread open in front of him, with Keelan mirroring the setup. He flipped through a few pages before beginning.

"Okay, boss. Facts. Two bodies, Melanie Nowak and Anthony Miller. Keelan dug into their history, how they met, their connection. Anthony worked on the legal team representing Melanie's employer, which is how they got involved. His close circle confirms he was a womanizer, and you, boss, verified that with Ann McFadden's story about his little stunt at the winery."

Julia nodded. That proposition at the winery had been the trigger for Ann's eventual call to Anthony. After Jack, Ann's brother, dug into Mark's activities and found something damning, Ann had put two and two together. If Anthony suspected his wife was sleeping with his colleague, well, his so-called friend, it would make perfect sense for him to seek payback by trying to get Ann into bed. Whether he succeeded or not, Julia had no way of proving. Ann said he hadn't. Anthony was dead.

Gustavo continued. "So we've got that romantic entanglement established. Then there's Daniel Nowak moving out of his house and into a motel. That particular motel allowed dogs, which is why he picked it." He paused, tapping his finger against the table. "Now, here's where we hit an interesting intersection—Mrs. McFadden's account of the encounter between Daniel and Mark Lancaster."

Julia raised a hand. "Quick detour. Make a note for me. Why didn't Ann ever change her last name to Lancaster when she got married? She's still going by McFadden."

"Gotcha," Gustavo said, scribbling the note.

223

He resumed. "So, back to the scene. Let's look at Mark Lancaster who, according to Ann, had been spying on her. We need to pin down his motivation for that. He and Daniel exchange words. Based on what we know, Mark should have assumed Ann was sleeping with Daniel. And again, according to you, boss, she wasn't. But we don't actually know that for sure. Anyways, Mark throws Ann out of the house that same day."

Julia cut in. "Bit harsh, don't you think?"

Keelan nodded. "Yeah. Feels too quick. But we don't know if that was the first time he spotted her with someone. Until we talk to him, we can't be sure."

Julia shook her head. "The guy is coming back from Boston tonight. His alibi is bulletproof. I triple-checked it."

"Right," Gustavo said. "But still, he kicks her out. Same day, she moves out. Same day, her brother Jack drops a bombshell and he shows her these." Gustavo slid a series of photographs onto the table.

Keelan picked up from there. "We analyzed both the prints and the digital files. They're legit, no tampering. Metadata confirms the timestamps. According to these, Mark Lancaster met Daniela Miller at least three times, same time of day, like clockwork. We checked every property in the building and nothing directly connects to either of them. But there are two apartments of interest. One's owned by a Panama-based company. The other belongs to a Boston lawyer who used to work at PPP, Pharmaceutical Production Partners, owned by the Wallen family. Same company that's a major client of Lancaster's law firm. The lawyer retired four years ago."

Julia let out a frustrated breath. 'So we're assuming Mark was using that apartment to meet Daniela. But without access, we're stuck."

Keelan nodded. "No judge will sign off on a search warrant for an apartment owned by a third party, based on nothing but a hunch."

Julia frowned. The apartment was a dead end at least for now.

"Let's move on to the choker," Gustavo said, flipping through his notes. "We have three major points to consider.

One. Daniela was definitely wearing it when she entered the office building. That's confirmed by security footage. When her body was recovered, the choker was gone. No sign of it.

Two. Ann McFadden claims she saw a photo of the choker's lock with an engraving, a letter 'M', on the back. The photo was taken by Anthony. But when we went through his phone, or at least his main phone, because let's be real, the guy probably had more, there was no trace of that picture. And so far, we haven't recovered any of his other devices. Might never, to be honest."

Julia nodded, absorbing the information as Gustavo continued.

"Three. The choker appears in Daniel Nowak's manuscript, described exactly as it was in real life. That alone is suspicious as hell. But there's one key difference: in the manuscript, there's no mention of the engraving."

He paused, then added, "We found the printed pages of the manuscript at Daniel's house. But here's the kicker—that version of the manuscript doesn't match the digital file recovered from his laptop. In the computer, it's not a choker at all. It's a necklace. The same version Ann McFadden remembers reading."

Keelan jumped in. "Speaking of the manuscript, boss, we ran a fingerprint analysis on the pages you found in Nowak's house. Two sets came up and one is Daniel's. The other is unknown, but I'd bet anything it's Ann's. We'll need to confirm. And here's where it gets interesting," he added, pausing just long enough for effect. "Fingerprints were on every page except one."

Julia raised a brow.

"The page describing the choker."

Julia folded her arms. "Could someone have tampered with the manuscript?"

Keelan nodded. "If we believe Ann who claims her copy vanished from her house, then yeah. Absolutely."

"So," Julia said, leaning forward. "Let's go back to the choker for a second. If the engraving is there, and it is the letter M, then that would pretty much confirm Daniela Miller and Mark Lancaster were involved. And not just involved. Most likely they were in a very specific kind of relationship."

Gustavo shrugged. "Maybe, boss. But I wouldn't overthink it. Plenty of people play their little power games. It gets them off. Could mean something. Could mean nothing."

Julia considered that. "Then explain why it's missing," she countered. "Because of the engraving, right?"

Keelan leaned back. "That's one theory. We don't actually know what happened to Daniela. Did she jump? Was she pushed? Was she made to jump? If it was suicide, she could've taken the choker off herself. Maybe as a final gesture of cutting ties with Mark, rejecting whatever they had."

Julia nodded. It was possible.

"But," Keelan continued, "if she was pushed, then whoever did it took the choker. And why? Because of the engraving. Which means Mark could be involved. Maybe he had someone take care of it. While he conveniently has an airtight alibi in Boston."

Julia tapped her fingers on the table, deep in thought. "That's a solid angle. We need to dig there. Pull every security feed from that building—garage cameras, access points, side entrances. It's a lot of footage, but if someone took that choker, we might just catch a break."

"Consider it done, boss," Keelan said.

"Let's move on," Julia offered. "Lab results."

Gustavo pulled out a report. "Confirmed—medical-grade sleeping gas, the kind used for surgical anesthesia. Lab says it was sprayed in small doses, likely to deepen their sleep rather than knock them out entirely. Then, soaked cloths were used to render them completely unconscious before the opioids were administered intravenously."

Julia's brow furrowed. "Would the person spraying it have needed a mask?"

"If they were careful a regular mask would've been enough," Gustavo replied.

She nodded, shifting gears. "What about entry?"

Keelan shook his head. "No signs of forced entry. Whoever did this knew the code. Walked right in. Only precaution they took was blocking the Nest camera beforehand. We pulled the footage. At exactly 4:13 AM, the system picked up an object, a stick, extending at an angle from behind the wall. Never caught the hand holding it, and then... nothing. The camera was blind."

Julia narrowed her eyes. Precise. Calculated. Cold. Whoever had done this knew exactly what they were doing.

"Anything else?" Julia asked.

"That's about it," Gustavo replied.

Julia shifted in her chair, rolling the facts over in her mind. "Okay, summing up. We have four suspects. Daniel Nowak. Ann McFadden. Mark Lancaster, if this was a pay-for-hire job. And Daniela Miller, if this really was a murder-suicide."

She turned to Gustavo. "Dig into Mark for any contacts in the shadow world, transactions, unusual travel records. See if there's anything off."

Then to Keelan. "Take Ann. Track her movements on the day Daniela died. Get me everything: surveillance, phone pings, purchases. I want to know where she was, down to the minute."

Julia exhaled, bracing herself for the next step. "I'll handle Daniel. Let's work fast. Once I have his statement, we'll pivot."

With that, the meeting was over.

Chapter 17

Grace placed the brisket on the stove, letting it rest. Ten minutes. That was all the time she had to gauge Mark before dinner.

He had come home minutes ago, changed out of his work clothes, and now descended the stairs. She watched him closely, searching his face for signs of distress. But to her surprise, he wasn't worried. He wasn't panicked. He should have been. Instead, he seemed... steady.

"Dad told me what happened," she said carefully.

"Yeah," Mark muttered, rubbing a hand over his face. "I called him when I learned about Daniela and... then Anthony. It's insane."

Grace leaned against the counter, arms crossed, her gaze sharp. "She killed both of them and then took her own life. That's big."

Mark sat down, pressing his fingers to his temples. A long silence stretched between them before he finally muttered, "No, Mom. She couldn't have done it. I know her."

Grace's expression didn't waver. She let his words settle, then, in a slow and deliberate voice, enunciating each syllable, she said, "She certainly could. And she did, Mark. There is no doubt about that. You got it?"

He lifted his head, meeting her gaze. There was something unyielding in her stare, something that made his stomach drop. A silent warning. A command. Mark swallowed hard. His chest felt tight, his skin clammy. A slow wave of unease crawled through him, sinking like lead into his gut. He didn't want to hear any more. He didn't want to be part of this. He wanted out. He wanted to be back in Boston, with Bella.

***

Scott, Laura, and Jack arrived just before dinner, filling the house with a sense of steadiness Ann hadn't felt in days. The moment she saw them, the tight knot in her chest eased, if only slightly. She wasn't alone anymore.

Scott pulled her into a hug, his arms strong and steady, but Ann knew he felt the tension in her body. He held on for a second longer, his voice low in her ear. "It's gonna be okay, pumpkin."

She almost laughed at the nickname. She was anything but a pumpkin now; both of them knew that. But it was from childhood, a relic of simpler times, when her biggest problem was scraped knees or a lost toy.

She smiled. "Thanks, Dad."

Jack was next, rubbing her back, his touch grounding. "Stay strong," he murmured. "We're here. The whole army."

She gave him a weak smile.

Laura wrapped Ann up in the kind of hug only a mother could give, holding her close, kissing her forehead like she had when Ann was little.

"Hey, baby," she whispered.

Ann closed her eyes for a second, letting herself sink into it. "Hi, Mom."

After dinner, Laura took the kids upstairs while Ann, Scott, and Jack settled in the living room with cups of tea.

"You were saying this guy, Daniel, he's in custody, right?" Scott asked, his voice steady but probing.

"Yes," Ann confirmed. "The detective told me when she brought Betty."

Hearing her name, the dog lifted her head as if expecting to be called. When it became clear she wasn't needed, she let out a soft sigh and curled back into sleep.

"Imagine that," Ann continued. "He was the one who found his wife murdered, called the police, and they still rounded him up."

"Happens all the time," Jack said. "Wouldn't be the first time a killer calls the cops to play the part of the grieving spouse."

232

Ann frowned. "I know the guy. He doesn't strike me as someone capable of that. He's not some cold-blooded murderer."

"That's a crime of passion," Scott countered. "People react unpredictably when they walk in on their spouse with someone else."

"That's not what happened here, Dad," Ann said, shaking her head. "According to Detective Ricci, both Melanie and Anthony were killed in their sleep by huge doses of opioids injected. That sounds planned. Calculated."

Scott nodded, processing. "You're right. That's different."

"So, what does this detective want from you?"

Ann's touch lingered on the rim of her cup as she mulled things over. "For now? Just to stay put. She asked me not to leave town."

Jack shot Scott a look. "Ann's obviously a suspect, Dad. Officially. They have to rule her out first."

Scott let out a breath, shaking his head. "Unbelievable, Ann. The mess you've landed in." His voice softened, but there was an edge to it now. "But it's okay. We're here now. Whatever happens next, we're not letting you go through it alone. I've already arranged for a lawyer. Alison recommended someone solid. He'll be here tomorrow."

Ann looked up at him, fear flickering in her eyes. "Do I really need a lawyer, Dad?"

Scott didn't hesitate. "Sure as hell you do."

They stayed up late, strategizing, covering every angle, making sure Ann was prepared. Making sure she stayed out of trouble.

***

The interrogation room was clean and cold, its only defining feature a large, dark rectangular window with a one-way glass, of course. They're watching me, Daniel thought, recalling every police procedural he had ever seen. Let them. He had nothing to hide. They had asked him if he needed a lawyer. Daniel had declined. He didn't see the point. He hadn't done anything wrong.

The door creaked open, and Detective Julia Ricci stepped inside. He had met her before. She had been there when they arrested him at the motel. She was the one he had asked to take Betty to Ann.

"Evening, Daniel," she greeted, settling into the chair across from him.

"Good evening, Detective," he replied evenly.

She made herself comfortable, studying him with the ease of someone who knew how to let silence work in her favor. Then, with a slight smile, she asked, "There's something I've been wondering—how come your English is so good? Almost native."

Daniel let out a slow breath, the unexpected question softening his tension. He sighed. "Oh, that? Well... I was obsessed with English." He leaned back slightly. "Back home in Warsaw, when I started my business, I hired a tutor, an American guy. Imagine this: three-hour lessons, every single day, for five years. That's how determined I was." He shrugged. "And I read a lot."

Julia was visibly impressed. "Hard work paid off."

"I hope so."

She studied him briefly before casually adding, "I thought you studied English at university."

Daniel nodded. "I did, but it was basic. My major was chemistry. I loved it, and I still do."

Julia tilted her head. "Then why didn't you pursue it as a career?"

"Money." His voice was low, depressed. "I couldn't find a decent job. Everyone wanted to be an entrepreneur, not a chemist. So I adapted."

"I see." She filed that answer away. "Right, Daniel. Tell me about this book of yours. What's the story behind it?"

Daniel shifted in his chair. He had been expecting this. The goddamn manuscript had come back to haunt him. He started slow, careful.

"Here's the thing, Detective. I had a business. An online platform connecting math tutors with students. It thrived, right up until Google killed it. Algorithm changes tanked my traffic, and suddenly, I was watching something I built collapse. I was desperate, trying to find a way forward." He rubbed his palms together. "I knew I had the skills. I knew digital marketing, social media, and traffic conversion. What I didn't have was a product."

Julia remained quiet, letting him speak.

"I started researching. Looking for that golden rule—low investment, high return. But online business these days..." He let out a humorless chuckle. "It's a nightmare to break into. It doesn't even matter what you're selling. Promotion costs a fortune. You need millions just to make noise. I didn't have that." He shook his head. "Then I came across self-publishing. And I saw an opportunity."

Julia's eyes narrowed with curiosity. "Go on."

Daniel licked his dry lips before continuing.

"My idea was simple. If I wrote a great book, all I'd need was an initial investment to attract the first thousand readers. And books... they don't sell because of ads, not really. The biggest driver is word of mouth. If a book is good enough, it sells itself. That's what I liked about it. I thought, probably naively, that all I needed to do was write something people couldn't put down."

Julia nodded. "Interesting. So how did you come up with the plot?"

Daniel hummed thoughtfully. "I researched. I analyzed bestseller trends. Liane Moriarty, Gillian Flynn, and Paula Hawkins attracted massive audiences. That was the kind of book I needed to write. But then came the hardest part: the story itself."

He hesitated for a second, then admitted, "And that's where I got help. From my neighbor." He let the words settle before adding, "Ann."

Julia's expression didn't change, but her eyes sharpened.

"Not that she knew, of course," Daniel clarified. "I noticed her on the trails. I saw her from my window, always alone, always with her dog. Something about her intrigued me. I started imagining her life. And then... I started writing."

He reached for the plastic cup of water, taking a slow sip. Julia watched him closely. Either he was a master manipulator, weaving a perfect web of deception, or he was telling the truth.

She was about to find out soon.

"I read the manuscript," Julia said, settling back in her chair. "It's impressive. But what I really want to know, Daniel, is your plot. Your endgame."

He smiled a weary, almost resigned smile. He was oddly at ease for a man sitting in an interrogation room.

"Promise you won't steal my idea?" His attempt at a joke was clumsy, but considering he had found his wife dead in bed with another man just days ago, Julia didn't expect much better.

"I promise," she said dryly. "I'm far too busy to read, let alone write."

Daniel nodded, then leaned forward slightly, his eyes bright with excitement. "Okay. Now, imagine this—"

His voice dropped, drawing her in.

"A woman. Trapped in a marriage she never really chose. A duty-bound life, tied down by two kids. She's desperate, searching for answers, trying to understand why her happiness is slipping through her fingers. The thought of leaving gnaws at her, but she can't, not really. The kids root her to the ground, but inside, she's screaming to get out."

Julia listened, unmoving.

"Slowly, her mind starts playing tricks on her. She begins to suspect her husband is having an affair. At first, it's subtle. Little things, tiny shifts. Then, it grows. Every glance, every late night at the office, every whisper of perfume that isn't hers. It all confirms her worst fears. And then she becomes obsessed. With the idea of this other woman. With who she is. With every detail, real or imagined."

Daniel took another sip of water, letting the story settle before continuing.

"One day, the news breaks—someone has jumped from the office building where her husband works. A woman. And she knows it's her. The mistress." His fingers tapped lightly against the table. "She digs into the case, hunts for proof. Then, she finds out that an expensive necklace is missing from the dead woman's body. A maple leaf with a huge diamond. The kind of gift a man buys when he's in love."

Julia inhaled slowly.

"But then—" Daniel's voice dipped lower, almost conspiratorial. "Something impossible happens. She finds that necklace... in her own drawer."

Julia's spine tingled.

"She spirals. She loses her grip on reality. The missing pieces start slotting into place, and she realizes the truth. She killed the woman. She took the necklace. But her mind erased it. A fracture. A blackout."

Julia muttered, "Jesus."

Daniel's lips curved slightly. "And now, she's unraveling. The guilt is crushing her. There's only one way out. She puts the necklace on, walks into that same office building, up to the rooftop, ready to jump. End it all."

A pause.

"And then," he continued, "her husband saves her." Daniel went silent.

Julia sat back, absorbing it. She let out a low whistle. "Hell of a story."

He shook his head. "Here's the trick, Detective. None of it happened."

Julia frowned.

"From the very beginning, the woman, Anna, was sick. Bipolar. The affair. The clues. The murder. She imagined all of it. None of it was real."

Julia stared at him.

"Except," Daniel added, his eyes full of sorrow, "for one thing, the necklace. That was real. Her husband's gift. To her."

Silence stretched between them.

"That's… ambitious," Julia admitted. "Must take masterful language to walk that line, to blur reality and delusion."

"Exactly," Daniel agreed. "That's why it's taking me so long. Every sentence is crucial."

She nodded. She took a mental note that Daniel seemed so consumed by his book, so lost in the world he had created that for a moment, it was as if he had forgotten he was under arrest.

"When did you first hear about the real fall?" Julia asked, her gaze steady.

"Ann called me. She was shaken. Said the manuscript had predicted it." He shook his head. "I told her to relax. That it was nothing but fiction."

Julia studied him. "Don't you find that coincidence a little too much to ignore?"

Daniel hesitated. "Honestly? Yeah, I do. It's unsettling. I mean, on the surface, it looks like a prediction." He paused, his fingers tapping lightly against the table. "Or... it could have been used as a blueprint. A scenario for someone to follow."

Julia narrowed her eyes. "And the only person who read it was Ann, right?"

A beat of silence.

Daniel met her gaze. "What are you implying?"

"I'm just asking what you make of it," she countered.

He ran a hand through his hair, frustration visible on his face. "I don't know. I feel like I'm caught between fiction and reality, and I have no idea where the line is anymore." He leaned forward, voice firm. "But what I do know, Detective, is that I didn't kill anyone."

"That's what they all say," she replied coolly.

A brief silence settled between them.

"You're really good at this, you know?" Daniel said, studying her.

Julia chuckled. "I'm good at many things. What's impressed you this time?"

"Making a man feel guilty even if he isn't."

She nodded. "Part of the job description."

Daniel let out a smile, shaking his head. "I've never been afraid of women with brains. Maybe I should have been."

Julia was intrigued. This man was different. He carried a quiet strength, yet there was an undeniable vulnerability beneath it. He was both emotional and distant, open but reserved. And somehow, none of it felt calculated. It felt real. Authentic. A man unafraid to admit his failures, to acknowledge his missteps without bitterness or excuses.

She caught herself. Her thoughts were drifting somewhere they shouldn't go.

Focus, Ricci.

She pushed the distraction aside and forced her mind back to the case, searching for cracks. Looking for the truth or a lie.

Chapter 18

Julia was led into a small conference room by a secretary who looked like she had just stepped off a runway and carried herself as if she still belonged there. Typical, Julia thought. These high-end law firms were all about appearances, polished and symbolic.

She declined the offer of coffee and settled for a glass of water instead.

Mark Lancaster entered precisely two minutes later, his face composed, though Julia could tell he was working hard to keep it that way. Whatever was brewing beneath the surface, he wasn't about to let it show.

"Apologies for keeping you waiting, Detective," he said smoothly.

"No problem," Julia replied, her tone making it clear—let's get straight to business.

Mark took a seat at the far end of the table, setting his coffee mug down beside him.

"I have a few questions for you, Mr. Lancaster, as I mentioned on the phone."

Mark nodded.

Julia wasted no time. "How well did you know Daniela Miller?"

Mark swallowed but kept his composure. "Well, she was Anthony's wife, so I knew her. We spent time together. Weekend getaways, family gatherings. We were friends."

Julia didn't nod, didn't react. She just held his gaze.

"And did you ever notice any hostility between them?"

"Not that I know of," Mark replied quickly. "They were a normal couple."

"Do you know anything about Mr. Miller's interest in other women? Ever hear anything?"

Mark shook his head. "No."

Julia arched a brow. "So you weren't aware he was seeing Melanie Nowak?"

His jaw tightened, but he shook his head again. "I had no idea." That, at least, was the truth, and Julia could hear the relief in his voice, the satisfaction of sharing something honest.

She pressed on. "You went to Boston Sunday afternoon, correct?"

"Yes."

"Why? What was the purpose of the trip?"

"I got a call from a long-time client. Legal issue, needed my expertise, so I flew down." He shrugged. "Happens all the time. They're my biggest account. When they need me, I go." He shifted in his chair, moving his coffee mug from one side to the other.

"I see," Julia said. "And when did you hear about the incident at the office?"

244

"Monday morning. My assistant texted me." He hesitated. "But we didn't know the victim's name until two days later, when... when they found Anthony."

Julia scribbled something in her notes, then looked up.

"Mr. Lancaster, witnesses say Daniela Miller always wore a black and gold choker. It was her favorite piece of jewelry. Can you describe it?"

Mark tensed. She noticed.

He paused, thinking. "Yeah... well, it was black with gold accents. A gold lock, I think. Honestly, I never paid much attention to it."

Liar.

Julia didn't say it, but she didn't have to.

"And, Mr. Lancaster, did you have any personal relationship with Mrs. Miller outside of family gatherings?"

"What do you mean?" His classic stalling tactic. Buy time. Get his story straight.

"I mean," Julia said evenly, "were you involved with Mrs. Miller romantically or sexually?"

"No! Nothing like that, Detective! We were just friends."

"I see." She let the moment stretch just long enough for discomfort to settle in. Then she delivered the blow.

"When Daniela Miller entered this building, she was wearing that choker. When her body was recovered from the car she fell onto, the choker was gone. It was never found." She tilted her head. "I'm wondering, Mr. Lancaster, where do you think it is?"

Mark's hands went up in a theatrical display of innocence. "How would I know?"

Julia studied him, unimpressed. "Right," she murmured. "How would you know…" She let his own words hang between them before closing her notebook.

"Thank you for your time, Mr. Lancaster. Please do not leave town until further notice."

She stood and walked out, feeling his stare on her back. She didn't need more proof. Mark Lancaster was lying his face off. She had achieved her goal. Now, he knew that she knew. Now, it was just a waiting game. Let's see his next move. Let's see what he'd do. The ball was in his court.

***

Grace and George were finishing their morning tea when the doorbell rang. Grace glanced at the clock — 11 a.m. Probably salespeople again, offering services she didn't need, from window cleaning to backyard maintenance.

She opened the door and found herself face to face with a neatly dressed, professional-looking woman in her mid-forties, with sharp eyes, the kind of official presence that carried weight.

"I'm Detective Julia Ricci, Toronto Police," the woman said, flashing her badge. "I'm investigating the recent incident on your street. A murder, actually." She offered a polite smile. "I'm speaking with neighbors, hoping to gather any useful information. Do you have ten minutes?"

Grace returned the smile, masking her immediate unease. "Of course. That tragic thing. Awful, just awful. We don't really know the details. Someone said she killed him and then herself or something like that." She stepped aside. "Please, come in."

Julia entered the house as George rose from his armchair, teacup in hand. He was a broad-shouldered man with sharp features that had softened only slightly with age.

"Hello," he said, offering a firm handshake. "George Lancaster. This is my wife, Grace. Please, have a seat."

"Would you like some tea?" Grace asked, her tone effortlessly warm.

Julia nodded. "That would be lovely if it's not too much trouble."

"No trouble at all." Grace disappeared into the kitchen.

Julia took a seat across from George. "I just have a few quick questions," she said, watching him carefully.

George nodded. "Go ahead."

"Did you know the couple?"

"Not really," George replied, taking a sip of tea. "They moved in about three years ago. Kept to themselves. They were younger than most of the folks here. This is an older neighborhood. I think I said hello a few times in passing, but that was it."

Julia made a note. "Have you heard any rumors? Anything at all?"

George shook his head. "Look, Detective, I'm not the kind to gossip. I barely talk to the neighbors next door, let alone anyone down the street."

"I see," Julia said. "And what did you do before retirement?"

"Lawyer."

Grace reappeared, carrying a tray with fresh tea. She handed a cup to George, then to Julia, before sitting down.

"Grace, do you know anything about those people?" George asked his wife.

Grace shook her head. "I'm not one for neighborhood drama. I had a couple of small chats with the guy, Daniel, I think his name was. From Europe, somewhere. Seemed nice. Never met his wife, though."

Julia took a slow sip of tea, her eyes sweeping over the room. The house was grand and elegant, with high ceilings, intricate chandeliers, and heavy dark wood furniture straight out of an English manor.

A massive two-story window stretched from the floor of the entrance hall to the ceiling above, towering over the front door. It flooded the space with natural light, making the already grand room feel even more expansive. A second skylight, positioned directly above, framed an unbroken sky view, amplifying the openness. And beneath it, as if carefully placed for the best possible vantage point, stood a stunning antique telescope, its polished brass fittings catching the daylight. The kind you'd expect in a Hollywood period film, meant for serious stargazing or perhaps something else entirely. Interesting, she thought.

"You have a beautiful home," Julia remarked, nodding toward the telescope. "Stargazing?"

Grace's face lit up. "George's passion. He spends hours with that thing in the summer."

"And mine is over there," Grace added, gesturing toward a sleek black grand piano nestled by another massive window.

Julia raised an eyebrow. "You play?"

Grace nodded. "My mother taught me. Then music school. I absolutely love it."

Julia let the moment settle before shifting the conversation. "Monday morning," she said, her tone casual but pointed. "Between four and five a.m., did you notice anything unusual? Hear anything? Anything odd on your security cameras?"

George didn't hesitate. "Nope. Nothing."

Julia studied his face for a moment, then set down her cup. "Alright. I appreciate your time."

Grace walked her to the door, polite as ever.

Julia stepped outside, her instincts humming. The Lancasters had given her nothing. But something about them nagged at her.

***

"Ann, are you sure you don't want me to drive with you?" Scott asked as she grabbed her keys.

She turned to him with a reassuring smile. "I'm sure, Dad. I won't be long."

She was driving the kids to Mark's for the weekend. He had asked to see them, and though every instinct told her to keep her distance, she had agreed. Grace and George were busy, and the last thing she wanted was for Mark to show up at her aunt's house. Jack and Scott would never hold back, and the situation could quickly spiral. This was cleaner. Safer.

Half an hour later, she pulled into the driveway of the house she used to call home.

Mark stepped outside as she parked. Mark Junior and Lily ran up to hug him before disappearing inside to grab their skates—he was taking them to the arena.

"So, how are you, Ann?" he asked casually, his tone calm.

"I'm fine, Mark. You?"

"Not bad."

The exchange felt oddly detached, like they had been divorced for years, and their only connection was the logistics of shared custody.

Through the open door, Lily's voice called out, "Mom, can you help with something?"

Ann glanced at Mark. "May I?" she asked, motioning toward the house.

"Sure," he said.

Inside, Lily was struggling with her water bottle. The cap had been screwed on wrong, and she couldn't get it open.

"I need water," she said, handing it over.

Ann twisted the cap loose and carried it downstairs to fill it up.

Outside, Mark lingered, watching her disappear inside. She was still stunning. Tall, blonde, striking, the kind of woman who turned heads wherever she went. A woman other men would envy him for. And yet, it had all fallen apart.

She could never give him what he truly craved. She was too independent, too strong-willed. Daniela had been the opposite—eager, willing, a plaything. But even she hadn't been enough. Bella, though… Bella might be different.

A part of him longed for his old life, for the kids, the family, and stability. But another part of him, the part that had always lurked beneath the surface, wanted something darker. Bella could give him both.

Ann placed the bottle under the fridge dispenser, watching the steady stream fill the plastic container. For a brief moment, her mind quieted. Just the hum of the fridge, the gentle clink of ice, the ordinary task of being a mother.

Then, out of the corner of her eye, she noticed a book. It was resting on the arm of Grace's favorite chair. It shouldn't have stood out. Grace reads constantly, always flipping through some bestsellers. But this book... its title sent a jolt through her.

Gone Girl.

Two simple words, yet they landed like a blow, heavy with implication..
Gone Girl... That's what she was now, wasn't she? The girl who was gone. The wife who had been erased, discarded, like she had never mattered.
Ann let the water overflow onto her fingers before snapping back to reality. She cursed under her breath, wiping off the droplets, quickly twisting the cap onto Lily's bottle. But her focus was no longer on the bottle. It was on that book. Slowly, she approached Grace's chair, drawn toward it like it had called her by name.

She picked up the book, turning it over in her hands. Was Grace reading this through the lens of Ann's absence? As if she had already been erased from this family? It felt deliberate. It felt like a quiet, triumphant smirk in the form of a book. Grace's victory lap.

Ann flipped it open, skimming the first few lines, but something else caught her eye. A folded piece of paper, tucked near the end of the book. Her pulse quickened. The paper looked familiar.

Ann wasn't the type to snoop. But this time, she couldn't stop herself. She unfolded it. She knew this paper. With shaky hands, she carefully pulled it free. One glance. That was all it took. Oh my God! It was a page from Daniel's manuscript, the one he had given her, the one that had gone missing from her house days ago. Someone had taken the manuscript. Now she knew who.

Grace.

Grace had been inside her aunt's house when she came to pick up the kids. She took the manuscript while Ann was upstairs.

Why?

But Ann didn't stop to think. She acted.

She grabbed her phone and snapped a picture of the page. Then, carefully, she slid it back into the same place in the book and took another photo of the book—evidence that it had been exactly where she found it.

Her pulse pounded in her ears as she stood, grabbed the water bottle, and headed outside.

Mark was still there, hands in his pockets, watching the street while waiting for the kids.

Ann handed him the water bottle, her voice steady. "Here."

Then, loud enough for the kids to hear, she called inside, "Bye, guys! I'll see you soon!"

Mark barely got out a word before she was already in her car, gripping the steering wheel like it was the only thing keeping her upright.

Her hands trembled violently as she punched in the numbers from Julia Ricci's business card, her fingers slipping over the iPhone keypad. Ann forced herself to breathe, steadying her grip just enough to press the call button. The line barely rang before Julia picked up.

"Detective Ricci," she answered briskly.

Ann swallowed hard. "Hi. It's Ann. McFadden."

"What happened?" Julia's tone sharpened instantly, picking up on the strain in Ann's voice.

"I... mmm... I found a page from Daniel's manuscript. Not all of it. Just one page. The one that went missing from my house."

"Hold on," Julia cut in. "Where exactly did you find it?"

Ann's mouth went dry. She gripped the wheel tighter, her pulse pounding. "That's the thing, Detective. I... I took pictures too. It was folded up inside a book." She hesitated. "Gone Girl. At Grace's. In Mark's house. It was her book."

Silence. A thick, weighted pause.

Then Julia's voice came through, firm and urgent. "Where are you right now?"

"Driving home."

"Ann, listen to me. This is important. I need you to meet me now." A brief pause. "I'm sending you a Starbucks location. Go there. Wait for me. I'll be there in thirty."

The line went dead.

The storm Ann had felt brewing for days was no longer distant. It was here, closing in fast, ready to tear everything apart.

Chapter 19

It was late Sunday afternoon when George and Grace returned from their weekend trip. They had flown to Montreal for the 70th birthday of George's old friend, a celebration filled with expensive wine and tedious small talk. Surprisingly, their flight was on schedule, and by 4:30 p.m., they were already pulling into the driveway. For short trips, George preferred leaving his car at the airport. It saved time and hassle, though the parking fees were highway robbery. As they stepped inside, the house was quiet. Mark was out, likely with friends. Grace headed upstairs to unpack while George made his way to his study.

Routine. That's what calmed him. He checked his emails, scrolled through messages, then pulled up the security feed. As always, he scanned the camera history.

Then, something caught his attention.

Ann's car. Saturday. The kids, rushing toward their father. Mark and Ann, standing outside, exchanging words. George narrowed his eyes and rewound, this time playing the footage at normal speed. He studied their body language, trying to read between the lines. Then Ann disappeared inside, probably called in by the kids. George switched to the hidden indoor cameras. The ones only he and Grace knew about. Every room had one. Even the bedroom Mark and Ann once shared. He had always known more than anyone in this house.

The kitchen feed flickered onto his screen. Ann, standing by the counter, filling a water bottle from the fridge's dispenser. Then she turned and looked somewhere to the side. Wiped the bottle, put it on the counter, and reached for the book, lying on the armchair, her movements casual, unaware she was about to detonate everything. She picked it up, flipped through the pages, and then extracted a piece of paper. A single folded sheet tucked between the chapters. She unfolded it, her eyes scanning the words. Then, without hesitation, she lifted her phone and took a picture.

The blood drained from George's face so fast he nearly blacked out. His fingers trembled as he gripped the edge of the desk.

That page.

The one Grace had carelessly left behind. She was supposed to hide it, for fuck's sake!

A single misstep. A small, sloppy mistake that threatened to destroy everything. All of it.

George shot to his feet, paced to the window, and stared into the darkness outside, mind racing.

Grace. She had failed him. She had been reckless. She had broken his trust. And now, because of her, he would have to fix this mess before it was too late.

***

Late Sunday night, Julia Ricci was still at the office long after most of the station had emptied. Since her meeting with Ann at Starbucks, things had moved at lightning speed. For the first time, Julia felt like the mystery was close to unraveling. She had called Gustavo and Keelan in for a final strategy session. Both men entered the meeting room, coffee cups in hand, sharp and focused.

"This time, I'll run through everything myself," Julia said, setting the tone as she flipped open her case file.

They nodded, waiting.

"Latest developments," she began, her voice crisp. "Ann McFadden finds a page from Daniel Nowak's manuscript inside Grace Lancaster's book at her house. Accidentally." She paused, letting the words settle before adding, "Or, Ann plants the page in Grace's book, then 'accidentally' finds it."

A heavy silence filled the room.

Keelan and Gustavo exchanged a glance. The truth was, both theories were possible.

"Keelan," Julia continued, "what do we have on Ann?"

Keelan flipped through his notes. "Still running through her routines, her routes. So far, nothing unusual. But I'm not done yet."

Julia nodded. "Gustavo?"

"Nothing that stands out," he admitted.

"Okay," she said. "Let's move on. There's one piece I can't shake. It could be something, or it could be nothing. But my gut tells me it's something. The fucking telescope."

She tapped on her tablet and pulled up a high-resolution drone image of the neighborhood. A drone-shot view of the gently curved street appeared on the screen. With a Stylus, she traced a deliberate line between two houses.

"Look here." She tapped Grace Lancaster's house. "Positioned at an angle to the road. And here," she moved the Stylus pen two doors down and across, "Daniel Nowak's house, on the other side of the street.

"This is the window you'll use for the telescope," Julia said, drawing a line on the screen. "It has an unobstructed view—straight to the front door. No trees, nothing."

She tapped the screen. The 3D model of the house appeared. "See this? The angle is perfect. When someone enters a code on the front door, the view is from the side, which means their body won't block it."

Gustavo and Keelan studied the screen.

"Makes sense," Keelan said with a nod.

"A partial but readable view of the digits. Give it a few days of careful observation, and you'll have the full access code." Julia continued.

Keelan let out a slow whistle. "Shit. That's smart. Simple and effective."

Julia nodded. "There's no way to prove it unless we test it ourselves inside their house using that telescope. So for now, it's just a theory."

Gustavo folded his arms. "What about Ann? Gut feeling, boss?"

Julia paused, weighing her words. 'It's tricky. But when I asked her if she'd be willing to play a role in our operation and confront Grace, she said yes."

Gustavo nodded. "That tips the scales in her favor."

"Maybe," Julia said, brushing her long chestnut hair aside. "We'll see."

Keelan shifted in his chair. "So, how do you want to play this out?"

"Here's what I'm thinking. Ann agreed to confront Grace while wearing a two-way transmitter," Julia said. "If Grace doesn't crack and plays it cool, Ann will also leave a listening device behind. That way, we'll hear what happens after she leaves."

"Makes sense," Gustavo said with a nod. "I'll prep the tech for that, a transmitter, a recorder, everything she'll need."

"Good," Julia replied. "Now we wait and see what shakes loose."

***

Grace stepped into the study. George sat stiffly in his chair, arms folded across his chest, his face flushed with barely restrained anger.

"You wanted to see me?" she asked, keeping her voice steady.

He didn't answer right away. Instead, he got up and paced the room, his silence making her uncomfortable. She waited. Finally, he stopped and turned to face her.

"Did you hide that page, Grace?"

She met his gaze. "I did."

He nodded slowly.

"Unfortunately, Grace, you let me down." He motioned toward the screen. She stepped closer, and her stomach lurched. There, in glaring clarity, was footage of Ann flipping through her book, pulling out the folded page, and photographing it.

"Holy shit," Grace whispered, color draining from her face. "I… I thought it would be the safest place… Oh, God."

She covered her face with trembling hands. The truth slammed into her like a collapsing wall, crushing, inescapable. She had destroyed everything. Grace stammered, "I… thought… Keeping it in a book I carried often would make it easier. I wanted to plant the page at Ann's place without raising suspicion.

George thought about it. Planting that page at Ann's had been a critical move, the one Grace never had time to make. She should have been quicker. She should have been smarter.

But he said nothing. He let the weight of it settle, let her feel just how badly she had failed.

A strangled sob escaped her lips. Slowly, she sank to her knees before him.

He didn't react right away. Then, after a long pause, his hand found her hair. He ran his fingers through it, gentle, almost soothing.

She wept softly, her shoulders shaking.

Finally, he spoke. His voice was quiet, controlled. "Time to go to the basement, Grace."

She shook her head, devastated.

"Please… I just… give me a moment," she whispered. "I..I feel sick."

George's fingers stilled in her hair. She didn't know whether he would pull it hard or release it. Then, after a beat, he pulled away. Annoyance flickered in his expression.

"Fine. But don't make me wait."

She rose and nodded quickly, pressing a hand to her mouth as if suppressing nausea.

She slipped into the kitchen, her fingers trembling as she reached for a scrap of paper. The pen scratched against its surface, silent, rushed, final. She folded it swiftly, pressing it into her palm as she retraced her steps. At the coat rack, her fingers slipped into the nearest pocket, her touch light but deliberate—a single movement, quick, invisible.

Then, without a pause, she walked toward the stairs. Head bowed, hands trembling.

Down to the basement.

***

Mark was drinking alone.

Sunday afternoon, he had dropped the kids back at Ann's, exchanged the usual polite words at the door, and driven straight to the bar. He needed it. The pressure was mounting, and with it, a growing sense of disorientation. And that conversation with Detective Ricci did not go well. He knew it.

He had never felt this lost before. Back when life was in order, when Ann and the kids were home and accounted for he had the luxury of indulgence. He could slip into his real world, the one that mattered. The power, the control. The carefully orchestrated sessions with Daniela, where he dictated the rules and she willingly surrendered to his dominance.

Taking Daniela from Anthony, his buddy, was a profound added pleasure. A satisfying victory. That was living. That was when he felt complete. But now everything was collapsing like a house of cards.

Daniela was gone. Anthony was dead. Detective Ricci clearly hinted he was a suspect. Ann and the kids were no longer there. Work no longer thrilled him. The future that had once been bright and boundless shrank into something small and suffocating. Mark swirled the amber liquid in his glass, then pulled out his phone. He dialed Bella. Voicemail. Again.

She had disappeared. Never returned his calls and never replied to his messages. Not even a vague excuse. He had left a few voicemails already, and this would be the last one. He wouldn't beg. Mark angrily tossed the phone onto the bar top. With Bella gone, what was left?

His mind fumbled for an answer, grasping for something, someone to blame.

A privileged boy from a wealthy family, perfectly positioned for success. So, how the fuck had he managed to wreck his life this thoroughly? Mark stared at the near-empty bottle before him, waiting for the answer to surface. It never did.

Chapter 20

The immediate hiccup in Julia's operation was minor but frustrating. Ann had called Grace's phone twice. Both times, no answer.

They decided to give it a few minutes. Julia topped up their coffee mugs and sat across from Ann. "I've always wondered," she said. "Why didn't you ever change your name to Lancaster when you got married?"

Ann sighed. "No real reason on my side. I remember Mark saying it was cool to keep my surname and give the kids double surnames or something. He kind of pushed the idea, and I only understood why years later. I guess his parents were against it. I didn't fit the image of a Lancaster." She let out a small, bitter laugh. "He even once told me I had 'village genes.'"

Julia's expression hardened. "He actually said that?"

Ann nodded.

Julia shook her head. "Wow." Disapproval dripped from her voice. "That's...unbelievable."

Ann shrugged as if she'd long made peace with it. But Julia wasn't sure she ever could.

"Okay, try the house line," Julia switched to the task at hand.

Ann dialed. This time, George picked up.

"Hello, George. It's Ann. How are you?"

"I'm good, Ann, thanks. What can I do for you?"

"I was trying to reach Grace. I need to talk to her, but she's not answering her phone."

"She's not feeling well," George said, his voice even. "Been in bed all morning. A virus or something. Maybe caught it in Montreal. The party was packed." He paused briefly before adding, "Can I help you with something instead?"

Ann hesitated. She needed to get inside that house. She needed to see Grace.

"Actually," she said carefully, "it's something I need to show Grace personally. It's urgent."

A silence stretched on the other end.

"Well," George finally said, "as I mentioned, she's unwell. But if you insist, Ann, you're welcome to come by anytime."

"Thanks," Ann said quickly and hung up.

She turned to Julia, her expression tight.

"He sounded legit, no?" Julia asked, glancing at Gustavo, who had been recording the call.

"He did," Gustavo admitted.

"So what now?" Ann asked. "Wait until she magically recovers?"

"No," Julia said firmly. "We proceed as planned. You need to get to her, even if she's hiding in her bedroom."

Ann thought for a moment, then a plan clicked into place. A way in.

"I have an idea," she said.

***

Ann pressed the doorbell. A moment later, George appeared in the doorway, smiling.

"You're quite persistent, Ann," he said.

Ann clutched a small gift box wrapped in festive Christmas paper. "I just need a few words, that's all."

"Come on in," he motioned her inside. "Tea?"

"Umm, sure," Ann replied, stepping into the kitchen. She placed the box on the island and perched on one of the highchairs.

George busied himself at the kettle, then glanced back at her. "I haven't checked on her in a couple of hours, got caught up with my own stuff, but before that, she was still sleeping. Said she felt really down last night. You know how viruses are these days, especially COVID. They can mess with your head."

Ann nodded but stayed silent. George was unusually chatty. She couldn't remember the last time they had exchanged more than a few words.

"I'll bring her down," he continued, setting three cups on the counter — one for Ann, one for Grace, one for himself. "Unless you are scared to catch a bug, Ann."

No I am not, Ann thought. I am not here to catch a bug. I am here to plant one. He opened the fridge, retrieving a glass dish of freshly made tiramisu, Grace's signature dessert. "Give me a moment."

As soon as he left the kitchen, Ann slid a tiny listening device under the counter and pressed it lightly so it stuck properly. Now, if she left empty-handed, Julia would still know everything said inside these walls.

A minute later, George's frantic voice echoed through the house.

"Ann! Come here! Now!"

She nearly fell off her chair, bolting up the stairs. George stood beside the bed, gripping Grace's limp hand. His face was pale, his eyes wild with shock. His entire body trembled as he barely managed to whisper, "She's dead."

Ann's breath caught in her throat. She stepped forward. Grace lay motionless. No rise and fall of her chest. No sign of breath. Ann reached for her neck. No pulse. The skin was already beginning to cool.

Then, something caught her eye. Behind Grace's shoulder, nestled in her dark hair, were two tiny pills. Ann gently lifted the strands aside. More pills.

She pulled back the blanket. An empty bottle of sleeping pills rested beside Grace's hand. Next to it, a single sheet of paper.

Ann picked it up, her hands trembling.

The note, written in Grace's familiar handwriting, read:

"I am so sorry for what I've done. I have let all of you down. I do not deserve to live. Love you, Grace."

Ann's fingers went numb, and the paper slipped from her grasp, fluttering back onto the bed.

The silence in the room was suffocating. George was motionless, his expression hollow.

Finally, Ann found her voice. "Call 911."

The ambulance and police arrived simultaneously, their flashing lights cutting through the evening gloom. Julia followed them in, taking control of the scene. George was escorted into an empty bedroom, his face pale, his breath uneven. His blood pressure had spiked, and the paramedics administered a mild sedative to steady him.

Forty minutes later, the front door burst open. Mark stormed inside, brushing past officers as they tried to contain him. He bounded up the stairs, ignoring the protests, and shoved his way into the bedroom. The moment his eyes landed on his mother's lifeless body, he froze. Then, his knees buckled. He collapsed beside the bed, his trembling hands grasping at her still form.

"Mom," he choked out, barely a whisper. Then again, louder this time. "Mom." His sobs broke through the stunned silence of the room.

Ann, standing nearby, felt a heavy and unrelenting pressure settle in her heart. Slowly, she stepped forward, placing a gentle hand on his shoulder.

"Come, Mark," she said quietly.

He lifted his head, his tear-streaked face full of disbelief. His body trembled as he tried to make sense of what was in front of him. For a long moment, he didn't move. Then, sluggishly, as if his legs weighed a thousand pounds, he rose to his feet.

Downstairs, Ann handed him a glass of water. He took it but barely seemed to register its presence.

"Why would she do this?" he asked, his voice raw. His fingers curled tightly around the glass. "What did she do, Ann?"

Ann held his gaze, her own heart pounding. She wanted to scream the truth—because she had killed Daniela, Anthony, and Melanie. Because the weight of it crushed her. But she didn't. She couldn't. This was something he had to come to terms with on his own.

Upstairs, the paramedics completed their work. Grace's body was carefully removed and taken to the morgue, where an autopsy would follow. The cause of death was evident, but protocol demanded confirmation. The law required it.

***

"What now?" Ann asked, her voice edged with exhaustion. The four of them sat huddled in a quiet corner of The Keg, assessing, recalibrating. "Is it over?"

It was the question Julia desperately wanted to answer. But she couldn't. Not truthfully.

"Look, Ann, this case is a goddamn nightmare. Nothing is certain. Everything we have is circumstantial. The swapped manuscript page, Grace's so-called suicide note. We still need to verify the handwriting."

"I'm on it," Gustavo confirmed.

Julia nodded. "The reality is, we could hit a dead end. It all points to Grace, but think about it. Was Mark involved? Was George? And Grace… was this really a suicide? Or did someone make sure she wouldn't talk? But then again, the suicide note. Would someone really write one willingly unless they meant to die?"

Julia's voice was quiet but firm. "We keep digging. Something will break."

Ann swallowed hard and nodded. She desperately wanted to get out of this, leave it behind, and disappear to Huntsville, to her old new life.

Keelan took a slow sip of his beer, eyes narrowed in thought. "I keep coming back to the timing," he said. "Suicide or not, that part doesn't change. It was damn convenient. Almost like she knew Ann had found that page."

Julia's mind snapped into focus. She straightened, her pulse kicking up. "Exactly. The timing. But how would she know? She was in Montreal on Saturday, and it's been verified. Mark was outside, according to Ann." She paused, and then realization hit. "Cameras! That's it."

She grabbed her phone, already dialing. "I'm calling the judge. We need a warrant now."

After a brief exchange, she hung up, her expression set. "Gustavo, Keelan, get back to the house. The warrant will be ready by the time you arrive. Call me the second you find anything."

Without another word, the two detectives pushed back from the table and strode out. Julia flagged down the waiter, settled the bill, and turned to Ann.

"I'll be at the office," she said, heading for her car. "You go home, get some rest. I'll be in touch tomorrow."

Ann nodded, but as she watched Julia disappear into the night, rest seemed like the last thing she would be able to find.

***

Ann was back at Aunt Meg's. The house was still, wrapped in the quiet rhythm of steady breathing. Jack and her parents were still there; they refused to leave her alone in this chaos.

But sleep wouldn't come to Ann.

She lay there, staring at the ceiling, her mind trapped in a relentless loop, replaying the day's events, searching for the thing she had missed because there had to be something.

Mark's face wouldn't leave her mind. It was etched with grief, raw and honest. With unmistakable pain. What did she do, Ann? The question still rang in her ears. He had looked blindsided, gutted. And Ann believed him. You can't fake that. Which meant Mark had nothing to do with Grace's death. And yet... neither had George, or so it seemed. His reaction had been just as shaken, just as stunned. Ann had seen it in his eyes, in the way his body locked up, in the way his words faltered.

So if not them, then who? Did Grace really take her own life out of guilt? Was she even capable of pulling off murders like that? Ann's gut twisted. There were no answers to these questions. The only thing that stood out was the timing. Too perfect. Too neat. And that could mean only one thing. It wasn't over. Not yet.

***

After consulting with the judge, the decision was made—Daniel was to be released. Julia wasn't thrilled, but the latest developments made it difficult to justify keeping him locked up. The evidence was too thin. The judge, who had initially agreed with her, now felt it was time to reconsider.

Before he walked free, Julia wanted a final conversation. She entered the interrogation room, carrying two cups of coffee. Instead of greeting him, she simply placed one in front of him. He took the cup, lifted it to his nose, and inhaled.

"Smells like Christmas," he murmured. "Thank you."

She allowed herself a faint smile. "I'm letting you go, Daniel. On one condition—you return to the motel and stay there until I lift the movement restriction. No travel beyond a ten-mile radius. Understood?"

He nodded. "Can I pick up my dog?"

She let out a soft smile. "It is definitely within ten miles, so, yes." She expected him to ask about the case. To demand answers. To react in some way to his release. But he didn't. Instead, he took a slow sip of coffee. Then, finally, he looked at her, his eyes serious.

"When this is all over, Detective, I want to go home. To Poland. Will that be a problem?"

Julia studied him. "Once the travel restriction is lifted, you can go." She hesitated, then added, "So you really want to leave?"

He nodded. "This life... this Canadian fall of mine... it's too painful to heal."

For a split second, she thought she saw tears threatening to form, or maybe it was just a trick of the light.

"It's about a sense of belonging," he continued. "And right now, nothing holds me here except memories I'd rather forget."

Julia understood the pull of home, the urge to retrace your steps, to believe that the answers lay in the soil where you began. She had been four when her parents brought her to Canada, immigrants chasing a better life. Italy had been their past, but for her, it was little more than faded photographs and stories told in a language that never quite felt like her own. And now, with them gone, she was alone, just like him, searching for roots, for solid ground.

But she had come to realize something: roots weren't just inherited. They were built. Planted wherever you chose to stand. Running wasn't the answer. Staying was the only way to make a place your own.

She looked back at Daniel. "Maybe home isn't where you came from," she said quietly. "Maybe it's wherever you decide to stop running."

He drew a deep breath and gave a slight, uncertain nod, but his eyes held questions he wasn't ready to ask himself.

Julia's detective instincts kicked back in. "And what about Ann, Daniel?"

He met her gaze, unblinking. "What about her?"

She leaned forward slightly. "I read your manuscript too. It seemed like you were... invested in her."

Daniel lowered his eyes as if suddenly fascinated by the cracks in the table. "It's all fiction, Detective. Just fiction."

He sighed, running a hand through his hair. "I need to find myself again. To recover. I need solid ground beneath me."

She understood that more than he could ever know. She, too, had lost her footing once. The man she'd loved had betrayed her. No children. No immediate family close by. The only thing that had kept her steady was her work. Her dedication. The cases that filled her empty spaces.

She snapped herself back to the present.

"I know the feeling," she said quietly. "I hope you find your harbor, Daniel."

Their eyes met. It was a tiny moment of silent understanding between two people who had both been broken in their own ways. Some things didn't need to be said. Julia wondered if she had met him in another time, another life. Would things have been different? This thought didn't exactly sit right with her, but she wasn't ready to push it away. Not yet.

Chapter 21

Jack had the kids all to himself, and they were making the most of it. They played board games, did their homework, and curled up on the couch to watch cartoons. He even introduced them to a few online games, with a promise that they'd say nothing to their mom. Ann was strict about screen time, and Uncle Jack was more than happy to be their co-conspirator. Mark Junior and Lily were in heaven, reveling in the rare, uninterrupted attention. With Mom and the grandparents out shopping and not expected back for a while, they had their uncle all to themselves.

Then, out of nowhere, Betty's barking shattered the calm. Jack glanced toward the staircase, hearing her nails scramble against the hardwood floor downstairs as she ran back and forth, her deep barks echoing through the house. He frowned and got up, peering out the window. No one was near the front door.

"Hey, girl," he called down. "Easy. There's no one there."

But Betty wouldn't stop. If anything, her excitement escalated. She barked, whined, spun in frantic circles, her tail lashing wildly and hitting the walls. Even Spike, usually more laid-back, stood alert, ears perked, though he wasn't as vocal.

Then, just as Jack was about to head down to calm her, he heard the crunch of tires in the driveway. He glanced out the window again. A car he didn't recognize had pulled in. Betty must have sensed it before he even heard it, and now, as the driver's side door opened, something changed. Her barking stopped. Instead, it became a sound so delicate, so full of raw, unfiltered joy, it nearly broke Jack's heart.

She launched herself at the door, whining, crying, completely unable to contain herself.
Jack knew, without even seeing, who it was.
He jogged down the stairs and pulled open the front door just as Betty squeezed past him.
She bolted toward the man standing outside.

Daniel barely had time to brace himself before she leaped into his arms.
"My girl... my girl," he murmured, his voice thick, as he wrapped his arms around her. They clung to each other, the man and the dog, frozen in that moment, her body trembling with happiness, her tail wagging so hard it seemed like it might lift her off the ground. She licked his

face wildly, whimpering, pressing into him as if afraid he might disappear again.

Jack felt an unexpected lump rise in his throat.

Finally, Daniel looked up.

"Hello," he said, his voice a little rough. "I'm Daniel."

Jack smiled. "Yeah. I can see that."

Daniel ran a hand over Betty's fur, his fingers digging in as if grounding himself in something real. "I just came to pick her up. And to thank Ann for looking after her. I'll never forget it."

"She's not home yet," Jack said. "But she'll be back soon. You wanna come in?"

Daniel hesitated, glancing down at Betty, who had no intention of leaving his side. "Thanks, but I think I'll head back home... I mean to the motel." He breathed out heavily, looking up again. "But please, tell Ann I'll call her. And tell her... tell her I said a million thanks."

Jack nodded. "I will."

He stood at the door, watching as Daniel and Betty walked away together. Betty was glued to his side, still wagging, still overjoyed, her whole body moving in sync with his.

Jack didn't know Daniel well, only what Ann had told him in bits and pieces, between everything else unraveling around them. A neighbor. A writer. A man who somehow got tangled in all of this without ever meaning to.

But as he stood there watching Daniel and Betty walk away, he realized their reunion revealed more about the man than a thousand words ever could.

***

The search of the house turned up nothing. No hidden cameras, no suspicious files on George's computer, and no cloud backups for the outdoor security system. Just a live feed with no recorded history. Inside, apart from the single listening device Ann had planted, the place was clean. It was frustratingly ordinary.

When they examined the telescope, they found one of the lenses was cracked.

"Yeah," George confirmed with a shrug. "Broke a while back. Knocked it over by accident." His tone was casual, but he seemed genuinely curious about why they even cared.

He had been oddly cooperative, leading them through the house without hesitation, answering every question. When Gustavo checked George's computer, he noticed something strange. The operating system was outdated by at least three years. But the inbox was filled with recent emails, and nothing looked suspicious.

"You should update your system," Gustavo remarked.

George chuckled. "Oh, I never bother. Not much of a computer guy." A doubt hit Gustavo. The man sitting in front of him claimed not to care about tech, yet he had an expensive, high-end monitor, which didn't quite match his supposed indifference. But with nothing incriminating in the files, Gustavo let it go.

Then, in the basement, they found something unexpected. Behind a mirrored wall was a hidden door. When George unlocked the door, the scent of chlorine hit them.

"Ah, my meditation room," he said, stepping aside to let them see inside.

The space was soundproofed and empty except for thick gym-style mats covering the entire floor. It was easy to clean. The walls were bare, the air eerily sterile.

"Meditation, huh?" Gustavo asked, his eyes scanning every inch, his instincts on high alert.

"Yeah," George replied smoothly. "Love to meditate."

There was nothing suspicious, nothing they could seize on. After a final sweep, Gustavo, Keelan, and the rest of the team wrapped up their search and left the property.

Back at the office, Julia fumed. Either she had been entirely wrong about Grace's involvement, or she was being played by an invisible hand. By someone who knew exactly what to hide and how to hide it.

***

Ann ended the call with Julia, gripping her phone so tightly her knuckles ached. Nothing. Nothing in that house. No evidence, no hidden cameras, nothing to expose the truth. "Even the damn telescope, my one solid lead, was broken," Julia said.
"What do you mean broken?" Ann asked.
"Yeah. One of the lenses cracked. George said it happened a long time ago."

Ann had kept quiet, but inside, her instincts were screaming. Lying bastard. She had seen George tending to that telescope like it was a priceless artifact, polishing every fucking inch with obsessive care. A broken lens? From a long time ago? Bullshit.

Frustration settled in. Julia was frustrated too, and Ann could hear it in her voice. But what now? They were running out of angles. Running out of time.

That night, Ann barely slept. Every time she closed her eyes, the questions swarmed her, circling like vultures. There was something she wasn't seeing, something just out of reach. But by dawn, she knew exactly what she had to do.

She got in her car and drove straight to Toronto. The city was a gridlocked mess, Christmas traffic turning every street into a slow-moving disaster. Over an hour later, she finally pulled into a parking space. She barely remembered the drive, her mind too focused on what she was about to do. Ann stepped onto the sidewalk and made her way toward the building. Two blocks in, she stopped at a traffic light.
The traffic light. Her stomach tightened.

This was the exact spot where a cluster of office workers had been standing that morning, waiting, chatting, sipping their coffee, when Daniela came crashing down from the sky.
Ann turned her head slowly, her gaze landing on the place where Daniela had hit the car. Right there. A dark stain still marked the pavement, barely visible unless you were looking for it. A wave of nausea rolled over her. Jesus.

The light turned green. Ann forced herself forward, stepping off the curb and moving toward the towering glass entrance.

She walked up to the front desk. Calm. In control.

"I need to see Mark Lancaster."

The receptionist barely looked up. "And you are?"

Ann hesitated, then made a deliberate choice. "His wife. Ann McFadden."

That got the woman's attention. Her posture shifted, her voice softer when she said, "One moment, please."

Three minutes later, Mark appeared. He looked tense. Agitated. On edge.

"What are you doing here, Ann?" His voice was low, cautious.

Ann held his gaze. "I need to talk to you."

He looked at her. Fuck. He didn't want to talk about anything. But standing there, he felt something twist deep inside him. She was so goddamn beautiful. Strong. Independent. The exact thing he had spent years resenting. And yet, right now, he caught himself admiring it.

"Talk about what?"

"Mark, we need to talk. It's serious."

A pause. A beat of hesitation.

Then, finally, he nodded. "Right. Give me five minutes."

They sat across from each other in a booth, the same one where Anthony had once hidden, waiting for the perfect moment to call Ann, anticipating her downfall straight into his bed. That moment never came.

Ann leaned forward. "I knew about you and Daniela."

Mark's reaction was instant—a flash of frustration, injured pride. "What?"

He almost went for the outright denial, the instinctive lie, but even he knew that wouldn't work.

"Yes," Ann continued. "I knew before she… fell."

Mark huffed out a breath, his fingers curling into fists.

"How?"

"Jack." She let the word hang between them, watching it sink in. "My brother figured you'd be the type to cheat, so he kept an eye on you."

Mark went pale, his face draining like death itself. His lips parted, then pressed into a tight line before he snapped, "That's illegal."

Ann's expression didn't change. "Probably. Doesn't matter now."

Mark swallowed hard, eyes darkening with something between unease and anger.

"Do you remember that day at Two Sisters?" Ann asked. "Anthony, Daniela, Julian, Jessica?"

He blinked, confused by the sudden shift. "Yeah... I do."

"That day, when I went to the washroom, Anthony was waiting for me when I walked out. He was waiting for the right moment. And you know what he did?" She tilted her head slightly. "He bluntly and openly offered me an affair."

Mark's jaw clenched. "Fucking bast..." He cut himself off, realizing how ridiculous it sounded coming from him.

Ann barely reacted. "I told him to fuck off. He actually looked hurt." She let out a humorless laugh. "But that's not the point. The point is, when I saw the photos of you and Daniela sneaking into that condo building at the same time, the first thing I thought was, 'Anthony knew about you two.' I was wrong. He didn't."

Ann shook her head slowly, her voice turning ice-cold. " I was the one who told him."

Mark stiffened, and his entire body became rigid. "Holy shit." His voice was barely above a whisper. "You?"

"Yes." She met his gaze without flinching. "I did. By then, you'd already kicked me and the kids out, remember?"

Mark's Adam's apple bobbed. Ann leaned back slightly. "Anthony was furious. You took his wife."

Mark snapped. "Jesus, Ann, do you really think I'd sleep with her? I wasn't screwing Daniela. I was disciplining her. That's what she needed."

Ann blinked once. Twice. Her mind stalled, then lurched into motion, her thoughts colliding in a chaotic tangle. Did she hear that right?

Her pulse pounded against her ribs, her breath suddenly too shallow.

She studied Mark's face, searching for something like guilt, shame, hesitation, anything that would soften the horror of what he had just said. But there was nothing—just cold detachment, as if he'd simply stated a fact.

Her stomach twisted. Not sleeping with Daniela. Disciplining her. A sharp, metallic taste coated her tongue. Jesus Christ.

"What the hell does that even mean, Mark?"

He scoffed, shaking his head like she was too stupid to understand. "You wouldn't get it."

She leaned forward, her nails digging into her palms. "Try me."

Mark's jaw flexed, his lips pressing into a thin line. His silence was worse than any confession. She had misunderstood the entire situation.

Daniela hadn't been a mistress. She had been something else entirely. Her hands trembled at her sides. Oh my God.

Mark was watching her now, head tilted slightly, as if gauging her reaction. A smirk curled at the corner of his mouth like he was amused. Like this was some kind of sick game.

Her voice, when it came, was cold. Hollow. Unforgiving.

"You really think that makes it better?"

Mark gave a half-laugh, half-growl of frustration. "Oh, come on, Ann. Don't act so righteous. Women like Daniela—"

"Women like Daniela?" Her voice was sharp, slicing through his words. "What exactly is that, Mark? Women you control? Women who 'need' your discipline? Women who don't get a say in what they want?"

She moved even closer, her face inches from his now, her voice dropping to a dangerous whisper.

"Did she cry, Mark?"

He stilled.

"Did she beg?"

Mark's nostrils flared.

"Or did she just stop fighting altogether?"

He didn't say a word.

Ann's eyes narrowed. She knew she would never know the truth. "Anthony swore he'd ruin you for it. But he didn't have a chance. Turned up dead."

"Are you fucking implying I killed him?" Mark hissed.

"No, you didn't. You were in Boston. Fucking convenient, Mark." Ann's voice was cold, measured. "You left Sunday afternoon, and Daniela fell the next morning, right after Anthony and Melanie were murdered. In bed. Both cheating on their spouses, by the way. No, you didn't kill them, Mark."

She watched his face. His eyes widened, his skin went pale.

Then she struck.

"But you knew exactly when to disappear to Boston, didn't you?"

"Oh, for fuck's sake, Ann! Peter called me! He asked me to come. He had this problem..." Mark's words cut off abruptly. His thoughts knotted into a maze with no way out. The beginning, the end, the middle, everything blurred, twisted, warped. What the fuck?

Peter had called him; that much was true and made it sound urgent, pressing. But looking back now, the timing was too perfect. Had Peter been involved? Was something unfolding right under Mark's nose?

292

Then it came to him. Mom was the only person apart from Ann who knew about Daniela. Cold rushed through him. Did she orchestrate all of this? Did she actually kill them? Send him out of the country to clear his name?

He swallowed hard but said nothing.

Instead, in a low, tired voice, he muttered, "Ann, I had nothing to do with any of this. I went to Boston at Peter's request to handle a legal matter. Period."

Ann suddenly shifted gears. "I trust you."

Mark's head snapped up.

Then she delivered the next blow. "So tell me, Mark, who did?"

His voice barely rose above a whisper. "I don't know. I refuse to believe it would be Mom. Not in a million years."

Ann nodded, took a sip of water, then put the glass down. This wasn't the moment to push. But she couldn't ignore the feeling gnawing at her, the way every lie stacked on top of another, building toward something she hadn't entirely understood yet. And if she could plant even a single seed of doubt in Mark's head, maybe he'd start asking the right questions himself.

"Mark, did you know your father's telescope lens was cracked? Supposedly a long time ago?"

He blinked. "What?"

"Did you know the telescope lens was cracked?" she repeated.

Confusion flickered across his face. "Who told you that?"

"Your father."

Mark frowned. "What the hell is he talking about? He used it recently. What does a fucking telescope have to do with any of this?"

"Good question, Mark. Why would he lie?"

He stared at her, trying to piece it together, but nothing clicked.

Ann stood, watching him struggle. "Think about it, Mark. Think about what's wrong with your family."

She hesitated, then added, "And be careful."

Then she turned and walked out, leaving him stunned.

Chapter 22

The lab results were in. Julia scanned the report, her mind processing every detail. Cause of death: An overdose of sleeping pills. The entire bottle had been consumed. Grace went to sleep and never woke up. No other signs of foul play except for two curious findings.

Faint marks on her wrists and ankles. Not glaring, but present. Traces of restraints, as if they had been used on her regularly. And then, something even more unsettling—small, fresh scars on her buttocks. Signs of... discipline? Julia let out a slow breath. Put these details together with the hidden basement room, add the missing choker from Daniela's neck, another symbol of control, and a grim picture of this family began to take shape.

What the hell was going on behind closed doors? A cult? A secret society? A carefully concealed lifestyle? And if Daniela had been involved too, what did that mean for her death?

Julia forced herself to refocus. Stay with the facts. What did she actually have?

The swapped page from the manuscript — gone. The telescope's lens—cracked, conveniently.

The house — scrubbed clean.

Main suspect — dead, an apparent suicide.

Mark — in Boston. Very conveniently.

George —nothing on him.

Ann—cleared, but not with hard proof, just circumstantial evidence and reasoning.

Daniel — also cleared. But still... not a hundred percent.

Julia rubbed her forehead. She had nothing but questions. No solid evidence. No undeniable truth. She made a mental note to get an update from Gustavo and Keelan. Maybe they'd have something she could actually use.

As if reading Julia's thoughts, Gustavo knocked and pushed the door open. His wild-haired head squeezed through the gap.

"Boss. This is urgent."

Julia motioned him in. "What's up?"

He set a tablet down in front of her. "This is the security footage from outside the main entrance of the office building. Time stamp: 11:44 AM, the day before the Fall. That would be Sunday. Look who's there."

Julia scanned the footage—people moving up and down the street, heading in different directions. Then, she saw him.

Daniel Nowak.

He walked slowly past the main entrance, watching the building. Studying it. As if he were learning its patterns. As if he were investigating. And then, just like that, he disappeared from the camera's view.

Julia's heart skipped a beat.

Daniel had said nothing about this. Which meant one thing—he was hiding it.

"Any other footage of him?"

"No, boss. Not yet. We're still digging."

"You do that," Julia said.

Gustavo took the tablet and left, closing the door behind him.

Julia leaned back, her mind racing.

What the fuck were you doing there, Daniel? Reconnaissance? Preparation?

***

Light snow dusted the cemetery as the temperature dipped just below freezing. Christmas was two days away, but for those gathered by the grave, the holiday felt like a distant, irrelevant thing.

Ann arrived with her family—Scott, Laura, Jack, and the kids. Mark Jr. and Lily stood in quiet confusion, still struggling to grasp what had happened. Grandma Grace had been fine, never sick. How could she just be… gone? They tried not to cry, but their red eyes betrayed them.

George stood apart, his face pale, hollowed out by grief. His sorrow ran deep, but it didn't spill over. Mark, on the other hand, couldn't hold it in. He sobbed quietly, his shoulders shaking. He had loved his mother. She had been his foundation, the voice in his ear guiding his every step. She told him what to do and how to do it, and she was always right. Now, staring at her grave, a kaleidoscope of memories rushed through his mind. The way she played games with him when he was little. The lunches she packed for school. The notes she used to hide inside his pockets, his backpack, under his pillow, little slips of wisdom, encouragement, love.

You've got this, Mark. Proud of you. Love, Mom.

Now, there would be no more notes. No more guiding voice. No more Grace. His breath caught in his throat. Oh, Mom… what have you done?

The ceremony ended. The casket was lowered. Final goodbyes were spoken. The grave was closed. Slowly, the mourners drifted away, leaving only Mark and George standing before the fresh mound of earth.

For a long time, neither spoke. Then, without a word, George reached into his pocket and handed Mark something that made his stomach twist the moment he saw it.

The choker.

Mark recoiled as if burned.

"I want you to destroy it yourself," George said. "So you know it's gone for sure."

Mark's pulse hammered against his ribs. His hands clenched at his sides.

"How... how did you get this?" His voice barely registered above a whisper.

"That doesn't matter, son. What matters is that when you take control of someone, you are responsible for them. For their successes and their failures. They are yours. And when they fail, when they make mistakes, you must act. Decisively. Because you are the Master."

A sharp gust of wind cut through the cemetery, but Mark barely felt it. His brain fought to catch up, to process the words his father had just spoken. Then George turned toward the grave and muttered, "Goodbye, Grace. You were good. Better than most. But even you failed me."

Mark's body went rigid. The realization finally hit him like a sledgehammer to the chest.

He staggered back a step. "Did you kill her?" His voice cracked. "Did you fucking kill her? Did you kill Daniela? Anthony?"

George said nothing. Just turned and started walking away.

The choker slipped from Mark's hand and hit the frozen ground. He didn't pick it up.

"Don't walk away from me!" Mark shouted, his voice raw with fury. He stormed after his father, grabbing his arm. "Answer me!"

George spun around, eyes flashing with raw rage. "Who do you think I did this for? Whose life and career do you think I was protecting? You would've lost everything. Your career. Your clients. My investment in you." His voice dropped, dripping with contempt. "You were weak. You failed to control your fucking wife, so you found someone else to bend to your will. And that was the beginning of the fucking end."

Mark's mind reeled.

"Don't judge me, son," George continued, his voice suddenly calm. "Go live your life. Be smarter. Find someone like Bella…"

He stopped. He had said too much.

Mark's blood turned to ice.

"What?"

Mark took a shaky breath.

"You knew about Bella? Oh my God. You set me up. Peter. Boston. Bella. That was you."

George didn't deny it.

The realization cut deeper. Mark's voice cracked.

"And then… and then you killed Mom…"

George waved a dismissive hand. "She had to go. She made a mistake. A huge…"

Mark lunged.

He shoved his father, aiming for his throat, but George stumbled back awkwardly, his foot catching against the uneven ground. He lost his balance. His body twisted. His skull struck the edge of a nearby gravestone with a sickening crack. Mark gasped. His heart pounded in his ears. He took a step backward, staring, shocked.

A dark puddle of blood spread beneath George's head. His eyes were open. Unblinking. Staring at the sky. George choked, his breath coming in wet, shallow gasps. His eyes slowly moved to Mark. His lips moved. Mark leaned in, just close enough to catch it.

"You think you're different… but you're not."

Then, nothing.

Mark dropped to his knees, his entire body shaking. He should check for a pulse. He should help. He should. But he didn't. He just sat there, tears streaming down his face, waiting for his father to die. He wanted him to die.

Minutes passed. Then, with trembling fingers, Mark finally reached into his coat pocket for his phone. As he pulled it out, something else fell to the ground—a small, rolled-up piece of paper. Mark picked it up. Unfolded it. His mother's handwriting.

Your father is going to kill me now. Stay away from him, son.
Mom.

Mark clutched the note in his trembling hands, his tears falling unchecked. He sobbed, pressing his mother's final words to his lips as if a kiss could bring her back.

Her last note. His last world.

And then, somehow, he forced himself to dial. The call connected.
"Ann," Mark whispered. His voice was broken. "I need you."

***

Ann sprinted through the cemetery, her breath coming in sharp gasps, the cold air burning her lungs. Jack was right behind her, his boots crunching against the frostbitten grass.

She found Mark nearly in the exact same spot as he had been an hour ago. He stood motionless. Beside him, sprawled lifeless on the frozen ground, was George.

Ann skidded to a stop. Her heart pounded. "Mark?" she called. "What happened?"

He didn't move. Didn't blink. His gaze was fixed on something far away, lost in the void.

Instead of answering, he slowly lifted his hand. His fingers uncurled, revealing a small, crumpled piece of paper.

Ann unfolded it. Her breath caught.

Your father is going to kill me now. Stay away from him, son.
Mom.

Grace's handwriting.

A chill crawled down Ann's spine. "Oh, my God," she whispered.

Mark's voice was barely there, a ghost of a confession. "I killed him, Ann." His lips barely moved. "I killed my own father."

Ann's eyes darted around. The graveyard was empty apart from them. George's body lay still, his head resting awkwardly against a neighboring tombstone. The ground was slick with half-melted snow, the grass beneath already stiff with frost.

She looked at Mark and saw George in him for the first time—the same sharp tilt of the jaw, rigid stance, and quiet calculation behind the eyes. This moment lasted only a split second, and then a grieving mask slipped back into place before she could truly see what was beneath—a shadow, a warning. He turned to her. "We need to call the police." She nodded, pushing the thought away. Later. She'd think about it later.

Ann forced her thoughts into order. She reached into her coat pocket, pulled out her phone, and dialed.
"Detective Ricci," she said, voice steady, "this is Ann. We had an accident at the cemetery. George slipped on the wet grass, fell, and hit his head on a gravestone. He's... he's gone."

She listened, nodding as Julia fired off instructions. Then she hung up.

Ann turned back to Mark. She slid the note into her pocket. Her eyes flicked to the ground — something glinted near Grace's grave.

The choker.

Without hesitation, she bent down and picked it.

Ann tucked the choker into her purse, the cold metal lock pressing against her fingers..

For a moment, Ann wondered if that choker had always been meant for Daniela or if Mark had ordered it for her first, only to lock it around Daniela's neck when he realized Ann would never submit.

"The police are on their way," she said, and stepped closer to Mark, touched his hand lightly, guiding him back from the body.

"Mark, remember, it was an accident."

Julia knocked lightly on the door. Almost instantly, she heard Betty barking, and a few seconds later, the door burst open.

Daniel stood in the doorway, his expression shifting from surprise to amusement.

"Oh, hi!" he said with a grin. "What have I done this time?"

Julia didn't smile. Instead, she stepped past him into the room, forcing him to move aside.

"It's not about what you've done, Daniel," she said flatly. "It's about what you haven't."

Daniel's grin faded. "Okay…" His hand instinctively went up to his hair—a reflex he never quite managed to shake. "So, what haven't I done?"

Julia paced the small room, then stopped, fixing him with a steady gaze.

"Why didn't you tell me you were at that office building twenty hours before Daniela's fall?" she asked. "What are you hiding, Daniel?"

His fingers stayed tangled in his hair. He let out a small breath. "Oh… about that." He sat down. "You know I was writing a book. Ann was my… my center, the heart of the story. Then, I came up with the idea of the Fall. I wrote and rewrote that piece a few times but wasn't happy with it. So I kept revisiting the scene, tweaking and reshaping it. But it still didn't feel right. I wanted to get a sense of how it would feel in real life." He shrugged. "So, I Googled where Ann's husband worked and went there. Made sense to me. Since I was already using Ann's personality, I figured I might as well use her husband's office for descriptions, too." He spread his hands. "It was nothing but the author's research, Detective."

Julia studied him for a long moment. His explanation sounded plausible. There was no way to verify it—but then again, they had nothing solid on him. Just security footage from the day before. Not nearly enough for anything. She knew it and came here for a different reason: gut feeling.

And now, looking into his eyes, she felt he was telling the truth. Or maybe she was getting old. Maybe she was getting emotional. Maybe something about this man distracted her and made her see him in a way she shouldn't.
Julia couldn't tell. And it bugged her.
She said nothing, just gave a slight nod and walked out, leaving Daniel sitting there, wondering if he'd be arrested again soon or if, this time, he was indeed in the clear.

***

Detective Ricci closed the case. The day after the tragic fall at the cemetery, Gustavo had another breakthrough. Hours of security footage were combed through frame by frame, finally paying off. A security camera from a neighboring building, angled just right, captured a glimpse of George slipping out through a side fire exit of the office building just minutes after Daniela's fall. A detail easy to miss. Almost too easy. That single frame was enough to prompt Gustavo to trace his movements. Soon, he found more. Another camera, this time from the parking lot of a building half a block away, showed George arriving and then leaving in his car. The timestamps aligned perfectly with Daniela's death.

The choker was still missing, but the evidence was stacking up. Then came another confirmation. Peter Wallen provided a statement that George had personally asked him to get Mark out of town. He had confided in Peter that the reason was Mark's separation from Ann, and Mark needed a few days to clear his head. That piece of the puzzle locked into place. The case was closed.

Gustavo leaned back and folded his arms. "What about the manuscript page? How exactly did that fit in?"

Julia stacked the last of the files, thinking. "My take is Grace was George's eyes and ears. She handled the groundwork while he executed the plan. They were a team, but he was the leader. The master." She let out an impatient breath. "So when Grace saw the manuscript at Ann's, something in it must have caught her eye. My guess is she thought Ann had written it. Maybe she believed it contained something useful that could be used against her."

She tapped the folder. "So she took it. But when she read it and showed it to George, they must have realized this wasn't just a manuscript. It was a gift. A perfect diversion. A way to frame Daniel. Or Ann, or both. It was too good an opportunity to pass up."

Keelan nodded. "And Anthony and Melanie?"

"I'd bet anything they figured out the affair through the telescope," Julia said. "That was always George's toy."

Silence settled between them for a moment.

"You never really know how sick people can be," Julia muttered. "The thirst for control, for power, it erases every last shred of humanity. And then… they stop at nothing."

She whispered out a weary breath, staring at the last open file—"I just hope that, at that cemetery, that was the final fall."

***

Ann woke with a start.

Her breath came in gasps, her heart pounding with the remnants of the nightmare. The room was dark, the air thick and unmoving. Her sheets were damp with sweat. She sat up, pressing her hand against her forehead, willing her pulse to slow. The past days had bled together into a grotesque blur. Grace was dead. Suicide, as they first thought. But it wasn't.

And George…his fall, his twisted body at the foot of the grave… No one would call that murder out loud, but it still was. The Lancaster family had disintegrated before her eyes, crumbling under their secrets, ambitions, and power games, swallowed by their darkness.

Except for Mark. Mark was still standing.
Alone in that house. A king without a throne. A man drowning in his own sins, gasping for control in a world that no longer obeyed him. What a wreck.

Ann shivered. She had been part of that family. She had carried Mark's children and had called that house a home. What had led to their downfall? When had the cracks started to show? Ann thought of her parents. Her family. Normal. Loving. Human. The Lancasters had never been that. They had been something else entirely. Not a family, but a dynasty. And dynasties had only one fate—to burn. And oh, how brightly they had burned.

She swung her legs over the side of the bed, pressing her bare feet against the cold floor. Tylenol. She needed Tylenol. Maybe it would dull the pounding in her skull, the raw ache curling inside her. She hadn't brought the bottle upstairs. She'd have to check her purse.

Ann reached for it, fumbling through the side pocket, her fingers brushing against receipts, lip balm, the smooth curve of a compact mirror— until they touched something else.

Slowly, she pulled it out, her trembling fingers closing around the delicate, familiar piece of jewelry. The choker. It lay against her palm, black velvet interwoven with golden threads, its elegant lock glinting even in the dark.

Daniela's choker.

Ann traced the lock with her fingertip, feeling its sharp, intricate edges. What did Daniela feel when she wore this? Did she feel beautiful? Did she feel desired? Did she feel safe? I doubt it, Ann thought. It had been something else entirely. A collar. A leash. A mark of ownership. Had Daniela thought it meant she belonged? Had it given her a sense of place, purpose, and protection?

Ann stared at the choker, her breath shallow, her mind churning with questions that had no answers. She swallowed hard. A thought struck her. What if she had worn it? Could she ever have wrapped this around her own neck for Mark? Could she ever have let herself be his?

She closed her eyes, and the memory washed over her—of wind rushing against her skin, the cold spray of the lake back home, the feeling of absolute freedom as she ran barefoot along the docks, nothing holding her down.
She had been a child then, but she had known deep in her bones what it meant to belong to herself. Now, holding this choker, she understood something else— some women were meant to be kept, and some were meant to be free.

Six Month Later.

The house had never been this quiet before.

Mark sat in his father's chair, the old leather worn but still carrying the weight of its legacy, the weight of every man who had sat in it before him. The glow of the fireplace cast restless shadows across the room. His glass of whiskey was half-empty, the liquid neat and undiluted because real whiskey lovers never tainted it with ice. He was slowly finishing up his father's prized whiskey collection, each sip a farewell to the past, a bitter tribute to the man who had shaped him and whom he, Mark, eventually killed.

His parents were dead. The house felt empty, a vast mausoleum filled with the ghosts of expectations, discipline, and control. The walls seemed to hum with their absence, the suffocating grip of tradition, rules, and the cold, structured life he had built on their foundation.

Since his parents' deaths, he had questioned everything—his choices, his life.
What had it all been for? The precision. The power. The control. He had built his world into

313

an unshakable fortress of dominance, obedience, order, and consequence. But now, sitting in the hollowed-out remnants of his past, he wondered if he had mistaken a leash for love.

Ann.

Her name alone brought the ache back. He had thought their life together was perfect. But perfection, it turned out, was a fragile thing. A mirage that shattered the moment he reached for it. He took a sip and rolled the whiskey glass between his hands. He remembered her before everything went wrong, her laughter, her fire, and how she used to push back before she stopped trying altogether. How had he not seen it? How had he not realized that her silence was not surrender but decay? A decay of their marriage.

Regret was a new sensation for him. Uncomfortable. Unfamiliar. But it was there now, curling around him like smoke, whispering in the quiet spaces of his mind. Maybe he had been wrong. Maybe, for once, control was not the answer to a fulfilling life.

Suddenly, a sharp knock echoed at the door.

Mark blinked, the sound pulling him from his thoughts. He gave a low, tired grunt, pushing himself up from the chair. The whiskey swayed in his veins as he walked, slow and deliberate, toward the front door.

Another knock. Sharper this time. Urgent.

He opened the door.

And there she was. Ann.

Standing in the door light, the night curling around her like she belonged to it. She was stunning. Devastatingly, impossibly beautiful.
A long, sleek leather dress clung to her, molded to every curve, liquid in its elegance. But it wasn't the dress that caught his eye.

It was The Choker.
The one he had always envisioned on her, had dreamed about it, but had finally given to Daniela.

But now, here she was. Wearing it. For him.

His pulse roared in his ears. His breath came shallow and quick, his fingers tightening around the doorframe as a shiver of pure, unfiltered power shot through him. She had come back. She understood now. Mark almost fainted as she stepped forward. Slow. Purposeful. Her heels clicked softly against the floor as she moved inside, her presence suffocating in the best possible way.

Then, she slowly dropped to her knees.

A rush of something violent, exhilarating, electric crashed through him as she lowered her head, exposing the delicate curve of her neck, offering herself up to him.

It was perfection.

It was control restored.

It was Victory.

Mark smiled, his fingers twitching at his sides, aching to touch her, to claim what was rightfully his, to correct everything that had gone so terribly wrong.

He circled her slowly, his steps measured. She remained on her knees, head bowed. With the faintest touch, his fingers traced the choker, then her neck, his thumb caressing her smooth skin.

"So, you've finally surrendered," he whispered, his voice silk and steel. "From this moment on, you are truly mine. Forever."

A tremor ran through her—excitement, anticipation, desire. He watched her shiver, her breath quickening. He knew she wanted him now, more than ever.

But first things first.

His fingers moved to his belt, unbuckling it. He slid it free, the leather whispering against fabric, coiling in his palm like a serpent.

She must be punished first, Mark decided.

And then…

And then…

And then…He woke up.

The room was dark. The house was silent. The whiskey glass, empty, still in his hand.

Ann was gone. Ann was a dream. Ann was never coming back.

***

Ann was driving the kids home from school when she turned into the driveway and saw Jack waiting outside. Standing next to him was Mark. "Your dad's here," she said.

Mark Junior and Lily lit up with excitement.

She parked, climbed out of the car, and said: "Hi, Mark."

"Hi, Ann," his voice was calm and measured. "As promised, I'm taking them to Disneyland. Are you sure you don't want to come?"

Ann held his stare for a long moment before shaking her head. "I'm sure."

He gave a weak smile, accepting the answer. "Alright, buddies, off we go! Florida awaits!"

The kids hugged her tight, then turned to embrace Uncle Jack, Grandma Laura, and Grandpa Scott before piling into the car. Ann watched as they drove down the long driveway, their excited faces pressed against the windows, waving until the car got out of view. She let a slow breath out. Her marriage was over. She didn't need to convince herself anymore.

Jack stepped up beside her. "Are you really sure, Ann?"

She tensed, understanding exactly what he meant.

"I am, Jack," she said, her voice firm. "It's better this way. We take separate paths. The divorce is settled, and the rules are clear. I have no interest in looking back. I only want to move forward."

Jack nodded, rubbing her shoulder in quiet support.

Ann turned her gaze to the lake, the sunlight shimmering over the water, the world around her in the full bloom of summer. A deep breath filled her lungs. I'm finally home, she thought. Back to my roots. Back to where I belong. Back to the village genes. A slow smile crossed her lips. She stepped inside. Dinner was waiting to be made. Life was waiting to be lived.

**

Detective Ricci was buried in paperwork, sifting through files, when a knock at the door broke her focus. Gustavo peeked his head through the opening.

"Boss, someone's here to see you."

"Who?" she asked without looking up.

"Kinda a surprise, I guess."

She shot him a look that clearly meant, Not now, Gustavo. I'm too busy for games.

The door opened wider.

"Good afternoon, Detective."

Julia glanced up, genuinely surprised. Daniel.

She motioned him inside. "Well, this is unexpected. How have you been?"

"Busy," he said, stepping forward. "Selling everything. Getting ready to leave."

"Oh, I see." She studied him for a moment. "And the book? How's it coming along?"

Daniel ran a hand through his hair, an old habit of his. "I deleted the manuscript. Burned the printouts."

Julia raised an eyebrow. "That's... drastic."

He gave a small, resigned smile. "Maybe. Maybe not. Writing and I need some time apart."

She nodded, then got to the point. "So, what brings you here?"

Daniel hesitated. "I, uh... I came to say goodbye."

"When's your flight?"

"In three days."

"So you've made up your mind," she said.

He held her gaze. There was something about her: strong, steady, self-assured. A woman with no pretense, no games. Just honesty. And it was that clarity, that ease, that made him hesitate.

"Yes," he said, then paused. "Unless..."

"Unless what?"

"Unless you agree to have coffee with me."

For the first time in weeks, Julia smiled. A real, effortless smile. It lit up her face, and for a brief moment, Daniel forgot everything else.

"I'd love that," she said. "Give me five minutes."

Julia reached into her purse, pulling out a small cosmetics bag. She needed a touch-up.

Flipping open the compact mirror, she studied her reflection. Was she aging? Looking worn out? Or was it just exhaustion settling into her bones with the weight of too many unanswered questions?

And then there was that feeling—a strange, undeniable pull toward Daniel. A gravitational force she couldn't control. Her university professor once told her: Pay attention to the pull when investigating a case. The detective and the villain are always two forces drawn together, circling and inevitable.

Was this that kind of pull?

Her mind raced through the case. Closed, officially. But nothing about it was clean, clear, or fully put to rest. Grace was dead. George had fallen. The evidence pointed to them— circumstantial but compelling. The security footage placed George at the building just minutes after Daniela fell.

But then there was the other recording.

Daniel.

One day before the fall, standing outside that very building. Watching. Learning.

This was the kind of case where the whole truth would never be known. Where justice, if it existed at all, had been handed down by fate rather than a jury.

Julia snapped the mirror shut.

Life… she thought. Life was a tricky thing.

In five minutes, she would be walking with Daniel to a nearby coffee shop, laughing, talking, and enjoying the moment. But she would also be watching. Listening. Digging.

Because with a man like Daniel, you never knew what might surface.

The End.

Printed in Great Britain
by Amazon

61847780R00188